Something moved again, making enough of a racket that he thought Blaine should've woke up.

"Somethin's out there," Largent said.

Blaine kept snoring.

"Denny, wake up!" He said. "Somethin' comin'."

Blaine snorted, but didn't move.

"Goddamn it, Denny—" Largent snarled, but he got no further. Whatever it was in the brush suddenly came out and moved at him with incredible speed. He saw large teeth, and two burning, yellow eyes.

"Oh, my God," he breathed.

He got off two shots—and no more.

Blaine came blearily awake in time to see Ed Largent's head bouncing toward him.

DON'T MISS THESE
ALL-ACTION WESTERN SERIES
FROM THE BERKLEY PUBLISHING GROUP

THE GUNSMITH by J. R. Roberts
Clint Adams was a legend among lawmen, outlaws, and ladies. They called him . . . the Gunsmith.

LONGARM by Tabor Evans
The popular long-running series about Deputy U.S. Marshal Custis Long—his life, his loves, his fight for justice.

SLOCUM by Jake Logan
Today's longest-running action Western. John Slocum rides a deadly trail of hot blood and cold steel.

BUSHWHACKERS by B. J. Lanagan
An action-packed series by the creators of Longarm! The rousing adventures of the most brutal gang of cutthroats ever assembled—Quantrill's Raiders.

DIAMONDBACK by Guy Brewer
Dex Yancey is Diamondback, a Southern gentleman turned con man when his brother cheats him out of the family fortune. Ladies love him. Gamblers hate him. But nobody pulls one over on Dex . . .

WILDGUN by Jack Hanson
The blazing adventures of mountain man Will Barlow—from the creators of Longarm!

TEXAS TRACKER by Tom Calhoun
J. T. Law: the most relentless—and dangerous—manhunter in all Texas. Where sheriffs and posses fail, he's the best man to bring in the most vicious outlaws—for a price.

J. R. ROBERTS

J

JOVE BOOKS, NEW YORK

THE BERKLEY PUBLISHING GROUP
Published by the Penguin Group
Penguin Group (USA) Inc.
375 Hudson Street, New York, New York 10014, USA
Penguin Group (Canada), 90 Eglinton Avenue East, Suite 700, Toronto, Ontario M4P 2Y3, Canada
(a division of Pearson Penguin Canada Inc.)
Penguin Books Ltd., 80 Strand, London WC2R 0RL, England
Penguin Group Ireland, 25 St. Stephen's Green, Dublin 2, Ireland (a division of Penguin Books Ltd.)
Penguin Group (Australia), 250 Camberwell Road, Camberwell, Victoria 3124, Australia
(a division of Pearson Australia Group Pty. Ltd.)
Penguin Books India Pvt. Ltd., 11 Community Centre, Panchsheel Park, New Delhi—110 017, India
Penguin Group (NZ), 67 Apollo Drive, Rosedale, North Shore 0632, New Zealand
(a division of Pearson New Zealand Ltd.)
Penguin Books (South Africa) (Pty.) Ltd., 24 Sturdee Avenue, Rosebank, Johannesburg 2196,
South Africa

Penguin Books Ltd., Registered Offices: 80 Strand, London WC2R 0RL, England

THE VALLEY OF THE WENDIGO

A Jove Book / published by arrangement with the author

PRINTING HISTORY
Jove edition / May 2008

ISBN: 978-0-515-14465-9

JOVE®
Jove Books are published by The Berkley Publishing Group,
a division of Penguin Group (USA) Inc.,
375 Hudson Street, New York, New York 10014.
JOVE is a registered trademark of Penguin Group (USA) Inc.
The "J" design is a trademark belonging to Penguin Group (USA) Inc.

PRINTED IN THE UNITED STATES OF AMERICA

10 9 8 7 6 5 4 3 2 1

ONE

The town of Rosesu, Minnesota, on the border of Canada, was in the grips of terror when they sent for Jack Fiddler. Fiddler, a Cree Indian, was said to have hunted the Wendigo—or the Wee-tee-go, as the Indians called it—and killed fourteen of the creatures. He was, therefore, in demand as a hunter. When he rode into town, he was met by the sheriff, the head of the town council, and the mayor.

The sheriff, Troy Dekker, did not approve of bringing the Cree in to hunt the creature—especially because he did not believe in the Wendigo. But he was overruled by the council and the mayor and was, as part of his job, expected to cooperate with the hunter.

"Jesus," he said as Fiddler rode in, "he must be a hundred years old."

Indeed, Fiddler had the appearance of a man much older than his sixty-five years.

"Just let me do the talking, Sheriff," Mayor Stewart Payne said. "We just need you to be here and to cooperate."

"Why am I here?" Adam Styles complained. "I got a store to run."

"You're head of the town council, Adam," Payne said, "that's why you're here."

The three men were standing in front of the town hall, where the mayor had his office and the council met. They knew the man riding in was Jack Fiddler. He was clad in buckskins, had a multitude of paraphernalia hanging off his horse—traps, weapons, the tools of his trade. As he drew closer and closer, he did appear to be aging.

"You're right," the mayor said, "he does look a hundred."

"Then you'll forget this and let me do my job?" Sheriff Dekker asked.

"No," Mayor Payne said, "we're not hiring him for his looks. He gets results."

"Yeah," Dekker said, "in Canada."

"Canada," Payne reminded him, "is only a few miles away, Sheriff."

As Jack Fiddler approached, they noticed that his chestnut mare looked almost as old as he did.

When the old Cree reached them, he dismounted and stood facing the trio.

"Jack Fiddler?" the mayor asked.

"I am Fiddler."

"I'm Mayor Stewart Payne," the mayor said. "This is Adam Styles and Sheriff Dekker. Thank you for coming. We've arranged for you to stay at the hotel, at no cost to you. The town will absorb the expense."

"I prefer to sleep outside," Fiddler said. "I will make camp somewhere."

"Oh, well, as you wish," Payne said. That was an expense the town would be spared. "Sheriff Dekker, here, will give you all the assistance you need."

"I need no assistance."

"You're gonna hunt that thing alone?" the sheriff asked.

"I prefer it that way."

Dekker exchanged a glance with Payne, who simply shrugged.

"Well," Styles said, "since Mr. Fiddler is here and we've all met, I'd better be getting back to the store."

"I will be requiring some supplies," Fiddler said.

Styles stopped, looked at Fiddler's horse.

"Looks like you got a ton of supplies hangin' on your horse, there."

"Mr. Styles owns and operates the general store," Mayor Payne said. "You can go there and take what you need, for free."

"At the town's expense," Styles corrected.

"Yes, of course," Payne said.

"How many have been killed?" Fiddler asked.

"Five," Payne said. "It was four when we sent for you, but it's five now."

"When?"

"Last night."

"Was anyone with the five people when they were killed?" Fiddler asked.

"Four of them were alone," Payne said. "But the man who was killed last night, he had somebody with him."

"I would like to see them both."

"Both?" the mayor asked.

"The dead man and the one who was with him."

"Sheriff Dekker will arrange that."

"And the other four who were killed?"

"They've been buried."

"Too bad," Fiddler said.

"You wanna dig 'em up?" Dekker asked. He looked at Mayor Payne. "I mean, since we're givin' him everythin' else he needs."

Payne gave Dekker an annoyed look, but Fiddler said, "No, there is no need to defile the dead. I will camp now, and then I would like to see the two."

"There's a clearing north of town," Payne said. "Uh, but it's a ways away from here. You'd be . . . alone out there."

"I understand." The Cree looked at Styles. "I will come to your store later today."

"Fine," Styles said. He looked at the mayor. "Can I go now?"

"Yes," Payne said. "We can all go now."

Fiddler nodded, remounted, and rode his horse toward the north end of town.

"You really gonna count on him to get this thing?" Dekker asked.

"There's a bounty on it," Payne said. "He's not the only one going after it."

"He's the only one we're payin'," Dekker said.

"Can you think of anyone else?"

"I can," Dekker said. "Fella rode into town today who would fit the bill, if he'd do it."

Payne stared after Fiddler, then said, "Well, I suppose there's no harm in having a backup. Who's your man?"

"Name's Clint Adams," Dekker said. "Recognized him as soon as he rode into town?"

"The Gunsmith?"

"That's right."

"Will he do it?"

"If we offer him enough money."

"We're already paying Fiddler."

"Well, if Fiddler doesn't get the job done," Dekker said. "I mean, if the old Indian gets killed."

"Well, talk to Adams," Payne said. "See what he says. See how long he's going to be in town. Feel him out."

"You gonna want to talk to him?"

"Probably," Payne said. "Who's to say his reputation is any more real than Jack Fiddler's?"

"At least he ain't a hundred years old," Dekker said. "And at least he's American."

"Jack Fiddler is American, Dekker," Payne said. "He's a Cree Indian."

"Could be Canadian."

"What have you got against Canadians, man?" Payne asked.

Dekker stuck out his chin and said, "They ain't Americans."

TWO

Clint Adams found Rosesu to be a very small, quiet, pleasant town. He didn't hear anything about the Wendigo until he stopped into the Border Saloon for a beer. All around him the conversation was about something called the Wendigo. From the description he heard, he assumed that the town had a crazed bear in the area, which had killed some people. Maybe a wounded grizzly or—considering how far north he was—a Kodiak. He'd seen a wounded grizzly tear men apart even while they were filling it full of lead. Saw one absorb a dozen shots to the body before somebody—himself, in fact—killed it with a head shot.

Finally, though, his curiosity got the better of him.

"What's this about a Wendigo?" he asked the bartender.

"Ah, that's some Indian myth about a creature that eats human flesh. Folks around here figure we got one out in the woods. You know what I say?"

"What?"

"Whatever it is, stay the hell outta the woods."

Before Clint could ask any more, the man took his beer-barrel belly down the bar to serve somebody else.

"I can give you some more information on that if you want," a man said.

Clint turned his head, saw the man standing next to him, and then saw the badge on the man's chest.

"Sheriff," Clint said, "buy you a drink?"

"The name's Dekker," the star packer said, "and I'd like to buy you one, Mr. Adams, and talk to you if you got the time."

"Time's all I've got," Clint said. "For once I'm really not headed anywhere. Just sort of drifting."

"Picked a cold time of year to come driftin' north," the sheriff said.

"The cold doesn't bother me much," Clint said.

Dekker signaled for the bartender to bring two beers. He scowled as he left them and the lawman did not takes any money out of his pocket.

"Actually," Dekker said, "the town's buyin' you that one, Adams."

"The town, huh?" Clint asked. "And what did I do to deserve a free beer from the town?"

"It's not what you did," Dekker said, "it's what you're gonna do."

"And that is?"

"Maybe save this town."

"For a beer?" Clint asked. "This I've got to hear."

Jack Fiddler made camp just outside of town. He did not go as far as the clearing the mayor had told him about. That would have been too far to leave his horse.

No, he found a likely spot closer, where the lights of the town might keep the Wendigo from coming near.

"You just stand fast, girl," he told the mare. "And if you hear anythin', you come a-runnin'."

He didn't tie the horse off. She'd be able to tell if something was coming for her, and she wouldn't stand around and wait to be killed. He'd had her for seven years now, and she knew enough to stand and wait unless there was danger.

Fiddler walked back into town and went to the sheriff's office. When he didn't find the man there, he changed his plans, decided to go to the general store for his supplies, and then look at the dead man and talk to the live one later.

Seemed to him the sheriff wasn't going to be as cooperative as the mayor thought.

The sheriff took Clint to a table in the rear of the saloon, vacated by two men when the lawman jerked his thumb at them.

"I've got to tell you," Clint commented, "this is not the best beer I've ever had so your story had better be good."

"Not a story," the sheriff said. "This is all true. We had four people killed last month by this Wendigo. Torn to pieces . . . and eaten."

"Eaten?"

Clint had heard of bears tearing men apart, but he hadn't heard many stories about bears who were maneaters. Big cats, maybe, but not bears.

"Maybe what you've got is a cougar," Clint suggested.

"It would have to be an awful big one," the sheriff said. "No, folks hereabouts are sold on the idea of a Wendigo."

"And a Wendigo is what?"

"A creature who eats human flesh," the sheriff said. "That's all I know. It's an Indian myth or something—except that myths don't eat people, if you get my meanin'."

Clint did. Real animals ate people, mythical animals did not.

"Okay," Clint said, "you've got my attention."

THREE

"The mayor and the town council insisted on hiring this Cree Indian called Jack Fiddler," Sheriff Dekker said. "I was against it, but Fiddler got into town today."

"So then he'll hunt this thing down, right?"

"I don't know," Dekker said. "I think his reputation musta been made years ago. The guy looks ancient."

"Fiddler," Clint said, frowning. "Fiddler . . ."

"You heard of him?"

"I think so," Clint said. "I think I heard he was a legendary hunter. I guess I didn't hear what he hunted, though. Wendigo, you said."

"Yeah, an Indian myth."

"But people in town believe it?" Clint asked. "To the extent that the mayor actually hired somebody to hunt it?"

"Look," Dekker said, "something is out there and it's killed five of our citizens."

"Then it sounds to me like you're lucky to have somebody like a Jack Fiddler hunting it."

"Me," Dekker said, "I'd rather have somebody like the Gunsmith hunting it."

"Whoa," Clint said. "I don't hire out as a hunter."

"Look," Dekker said, "you're in town, you got no place else to go—you said it yerself. How about just givin' us a hand?"

"Are you going to go out hunting it?" Clint asked.

"I was going to go with Fiddler," Dekker said. "It's the mayor's idea."

"And?"

"The old Indian doesn't want me," Dekker said. "Says he hunts alone."

"My question still stands then," Clint repeated. "Are you going after it?"

"Well . . . it's my job," Dekker said, "but I don't want to get shot by accident by some Indian who can't see."

"Who says he can't see?"

"I tol' you," Dekker said, "he's old, he's ancient."

"I think you're wrong to judge him by his appearance," Clint said. "Why don't you give him a chance?"

"Because he'll probably get himself killed, and some other people as well. This town needs a real hunter."

"I told you," Clint said, "I'm not a hunter."

"I am."

They both looked up to see who had spoken. The woman was wearing dusty trail clothes and looked like she'd just ridden in. She had long blond hair that was a rat's nest of dirt and twigs at the moment, and she didn't smell too sweet. Clint tried to look beneath the dirt on her face for her age, came up with thirty-five or so.

"Sorry," she said, "couldn't help overhearin' ya. I jus' got into town, came in here for a drink, heard what you were talkin' about. The Wendigo, right?"

"That's right," Dekker said. "Miss—"

"Don't call me *Miss*," she said. "I'm just Dakota."

"Dakota what?" Clint asked.

She looked at him and said, "Just Dakota. Do I understand that you refuse to hunt for the Wendigo?"

"It's not my job," Clint said, "and I don't intend to make a hobby of it. So the answer is yes, I'm not going to go hunting for a mythical creature who eats human flesh."

She dismissed Clint and looked at the sheriff.

"I'll hunt it for ya."

"What makes you think you can do that?" Dekker asked.

"I've hunted everything that can walk or crawl," she said. "I've killed snakes, big cats, and bears. I ain't afraid of anything."

"Have you had your drink yet?" Clint asked.

"It's over there on the bar," she said, indicating a hardly touched mug of beer.

"Well, go and get it, Dakota, and come join us," Clint said. "I want to hear all about you."

"Sure thing," she said.

As she went to the bar for her beer, the sheriff asked, "What are you doin'?"

"This woman is a hunter," Clint said.

"How can you tell?" Dekker asked. "How can you even tell she's a woman beneath all that dirt?"

"Look, you're complaining about how old Fiddler is," Clint said. "This woman has to be about half his age. Check her out if you want. Ask her for references, send a couple of telegrams, see what you find out." Clint looked up and watched her walk back. "I think she's for real."

"I don't know," Dekker said.

"Come on, Sheriff," Clint said. "She even smells like a bear, doesn't she?"

FOUR

Dakota pulled a chair over, slapped her beer down on the table, set her rifle down, and sat. She was wearing a gun belt across her chest, fully loaded with shells that Clint was sure would fit either the rifle or the gun she wore on her waist. She wore it high up, clearly not in position for a fast draw, but then a hunter wouldn't need that. She wore her gun simply as a pistoleer, not as a gunfighter.

"How many has this thing killed?" she asked.

"Five," the sheriff said. "The last one was yesterday."

"Was anybody with the victims? Anybody who might have seen it?"

Dekker looked at Clint, and Clint got the idea that Jack Fiddler had asked the same questions.

"The first four victims were alone," Dekker said. "Yesterday's was with someone, yeah."

"I'll have to see the dead man and talk to the live one," she said.

"That can be arranged."

"How much is the bounty, by the way?"

"Five hundred."

"That's all?"

"That's how much it was before yesterday," Dekker said. "I don't set it, and I don't know if it's gonna change."

She drank some beer, wiped her mouth on her sleeve. Upon closer inspection Clint thought she'd be an attractive woman if she were cleaned up. She was tall and solidly built, and her hair, once clean, would probably be the color of wheat.

"And how much are you payin' Jack Fiddler?"

"You know about Fiddler?"

"Anybody who's ever hunted a critter knows about Fiddler," she said. "He ain't hunted nothing but Wendigos for a while, but he's hunted every creature there ever was."

"Recently?" Dekker asked.

"Hell, yeah, recently. He ain't stopped huntin'."

"You got any idea how old he is?"

"Damned if I know. Sixty? Eighty? All I know is the man's a damned good hunter."

"Better than you?"

"Better than anybody."

"So why should we hire you, then?"

"Well, first off ya ain't hirin' me, I'm goin' after the bounty," she said. "Second, if ya do wanna hire me that's another story. Third, ya must not be happy with Jack because you was tryin' ta hire this jasper. So why not me?"

"Do you know who this jasper is?" Dekker asked.

She was drinking from her mug when he asked, so

she wiped her mouth again and said, "I musta missed that part of yer conversation."

"This is Clint Adams."

"Am I supposed ta know who that—wait a minute."

Dekker did wait a minute, while Clint just sat back and watched the two of them, amused by the byplay.

"The Gunsmith?"

"That's right," Dekker said, "the Gunsmith."

"Hell," she said, "his rep ain't got nothin' ta do with huntin'." She turned to Clint. "No offense meant to ya."

"None taken," he said. "I was just telling the sheriff the same thing."

"He can shoot," Dekker said, "better than anybody livin'. That's all I care about."

"He can't shoot better than me," she said. "I bet he can't shoot better than Fiddler. Faster maybe, but not better."

"She might be right," Clint said.

Dekker gave him a look that said: "You're not helping."

"Anybody want another beer?" Clint asked.

Fiddler picked out the supplies he needed. As Styles made a list, he frowned at each item. He wondered how long it would take him to get his money from the town.

"Is that all?"

"I'll need some ammunition—"

"There's a gun shop in town," Styles was quick to point out. "It might be able to help you better."

Fiddler stared at the man, then nodded and said, "You may be right. That's all, then."

"When will you need it by?"

"Tomorrow morning?"

"I'll have it ready," Styles said. "What time?"

"I would like to get started at first light," Fiddler said. "I could pick up the supplies tonight—"

"No need," Styles assured him. "I'll be here and I'll have everything ready."

"I am in your debt," Fiddler said.

No, you're not, Styles thought as the Cree left his store, *but the town is.*

FIVE

"So if you're after the bounty, why talk to me?" Sheriff Dekker was asking when Clint returned with beers for all of them. This time he paid the bartender, which made the man smile.

Dakota shrugged and said, "I thought maybe I could get more if I was hired private."

"Well, if what you're tellin' me about Fiddler is true," Dekker said, "then maybe we have hired the right man."

"So then you ain't gonna keep tryin' ta hire this Gunsmith fella?" she asked.

"Clint," he said.

"Huh?" She looked at him.

"You can call me Clint, Dakota."

She turned her head back to Dekker.

"You ain't gonna keep tryin' ta hire Clint, neither?" she asked.

"I can't hire anybody," he said. "I'm just the sheriff."

"Who should I be talkin' ta, then?" she asked.

"The mayor, I guess," Dekker said. He stood up, grabbed his mug, and drank half of it. "I gotta make my rounds. Clint, think it over."

"I'll think it over, too," Dakota said.

"There's nothin' for you to think—oh, forget it."

Dekker stalked out.

"You got under his skin," Clint said.

"That what you were lookin' all funny about?" she asked.

"Amused," Clint said. "I was lookin' amused."

"A-mused," she repeated, saying it like she'd never said it before. "That mean funny?"

"That means I found what you were doing to the sheriff funny, yes."

"Talk ta the mayor." Dakota shook her head. "I think he was funnin' me. Why would the mayor of a town talk to me?"

"Maybe because he wants this thing killed," Clint said.

"He's already got Fiddler, he ain't about ta pay me, too."

"He might, if you approach him right."

"You sayin' you know how ta approach him right?"

"I might be saying that."

She leaned her elbows on the table.

"When will ya know if that's what yer sayin'?"

"Maybe," he replied, "after you take a bath."

Fiddler entered the livery stable.

"I need a packhorse."

Ed Stack looked Fiddler up and down.

"You that Indian feller they hired ta kill that Windy-go?"

"Wendigo," Fiddler said. "Yes."

"Hellfire, man, yer as old as me."

Fiddler smiled for the first time since he rode into town.

"Probably older," he said.

"Kin you even sit a horse?"

"For hours," Fiddler said.

Stack looked him up and down again.

"Yeah, maybe ya can at that," Stack said. "Well, come on, I got orders ta give you what you want. Town's supposed ta pay me back but it prolly ain't never gonna happen."

Fiddler didn't feel bad about that. Whenever he was hired by someone—a person, a group, or a town—the details of how he got outfitted and paid were up to them. He didn't fret about that sort of thing, especially when it came to town politics.

He followed the liveryman out the back door to the corral.

"Why the hell would I wanna take a bath?" Dakota asked.

"So I could see the woman underneath all the dirt."

Dakota touched her hair before she caught herself and lowered her hand.

"Well, of course, I was gonna take a bath," she said. "First I wanted ta get a drink to cut the dust, then a room, and then a bath." She hesitated, then added, "I know I'm dirty, Mr. Gunsmith."

"Clint," he said, "just Clint."

"Yeah, okay, Clint," she said. "So yer sayin' you'll help me with the mayor after I take a bath?"

"I don't know the mayor," Clint said, "but if they're looking to hire me, I can probably get in to see him. I can put a good word in for you."

"Why would you do that?"

"Because I don't want to hunt for this thing," he said.

"You scared?"

"I've hunted animals before," he said. "When they kill, they usually kill to survive—or because they're cornered."

"That's true enough."

"I don't know the whole story with this thing," he said. "And I didn't come here looking for a job hunting a crazed animal. You did, and you look like you've done it before."

"I have."

"What about Fiddler?""

"What about him?"

"How's he going to feel about you trying to take his job?" he asked.

"Fiddler knows it's open season on . . . on whatever's out there. He'll understand."

"Do you think it's a Wendigo?"

"Beats me."

"Have you ever seen a Wendigo?"

"I haven't," she said. "But Fiddler's seen 'em, and killed 'em."

"So you believe in these creatures?"

"I believe there's somethin' out there that deserves

killin'," she said, "and it has a price on its head. That's all I gotta know."

"Okay, then."

"Okay."

She stared at him, playing with her half-full beer mug.

"Which of these hotels has got baths?" she asked.

"I'm in the Northwood Hotel," he said. "I believe they have facilities."

"Yeah," she said, "okay." She finished her beer, slammed the empty mug down on the chair. "Gotta take care of my horse first."

"I'm not in a hurry," he said. "I don't think anybody's going out after this thing until tomorrow."

"We'll," she said, "I'll see ya after I take care of my animal, get a room, and, uh, take a bath."

"I'll be right here," he assured her.

He watched her walk out, and realized that from behind—wearing a man's shirt and trousers—she cut an impressive figure. He was very interested to see what the bath was going to reveal underneath all that grime.

SIX

Fiddler picked out his packhorse. To the surprise of the liveryman—who told Fiddler just to call him 'ol Jed—the Cree did not pick out one of the better, more expensive horses. He took a ten-year-old nag that stack was thinking about gettin' rid of.

"Why that one?" Stack asked Fiddler. "It'll likely get ya where yer goin', but it won't get ya back."

"I am hunting a Wendigo," Fiddler said. "I do not expect this horse to survive."

"Ya mean ya expect it to get eaten?"

"I hope it does."

"Oh, I get it," Stack said. "Yer usin' it as a pack animal, but yer also usin' it fer bait."

"I will pick it up in the morning," Fiddler said.

"Sure thing," Stack said. "I'm here at first light, anyway."

Fiddler nodded and left the livery. His next stop—what was to be his first, but was now his last—was the sheriff's office.

• • •

Dakota was on her way to the livery, walking her horse, when she saw Fiddler coming toward her.

They stopped in the middle of the street to talk.

"Hey, Fiddler."

The old Cree did not look surprised to see her.

"Dakota," he said, nodding.

"Not surprised?"

"No," he said. "I would have been surprised if you had not come."

"Where ya off to?"

"The sheriff's office," Fiddler said, "although I do not think the man means to be very cooperative."

"I don't think so either," she said. "He was just in the saloon tryin' to talk Clint Adams into goin' huntin'."

"Clint Adams?" Fiddler said. "He does not hunt."

"For the right amount of money, anybody hunts, Fiddler," she said, "but so far Adams ain't bitin'."

"Are you goin' out alone?" Fiddler asked her.

"Unless you wanna take me with you."

"I hunt alone," he said. "You know that."

"Yeah, I know," she said. "Then I guess I'll be goin' out alone."

"You should not hunt the Wendigo, Dakota," Fiddler said. "You are not experienced."

"I'm an experienced hunter, Jack," she said. "You know that."

"But you have not hunted the Wendigo."

"Can it be killed?"

"Yes, but—"

"Then I can hunt it, and I can kill it. I need the money, Jack," she said.

"I understand."

"I gotta take care of my horse and get me a room," she said. "You camped out?"

"North of town."

"I'll come have some coffee with you."

"I would like that."

The two friendly competitors continued on their way.

Fiddler entered the sheriff's office, found the man sitting behind his desk.

"There ya are," Dekker said. "Thought ya forgot about me."

"I stopped in earlier, but you were not here."

"Musta been makin' my rounds. You get the supplies you needed from Styles?"

"Yes, and a packhorse from the livery. Now I need to pick up some ammunition from the gun shop, and perhaps another weapon," Fiddler explained.

"What can I do for ya, then?"

Fiddler gave it some thought.

"I think all I require of you is to stop Dakota from trying to hunt the Wendigo."

"Now how can I do that?" Dekker said. "That lady's got as much right to try for the bounty as anyone."

"Remove the bounty," Fiddler said. "Now that I am here, you do not need a bunch of amateur hunters out there, perhaps shooting each other."

"You're probably right about that, but she don't seem like no amateur."

"When it comes to this, she is."

"Far as this beast is concerned, you think you're the only one who ain't an amateur, ain't that right?"

"My ancestors hunted it, and I hunt it."

"I'll talk to the mayor about takin' off the bounty," Dekker said. "You don't need the amateurs out there shootin' at you. That's about all I can do, though."

"Very well," Fiddler said. "I will accept whatever help you offer."

"You get settled in camp?"

"Yes."

"Didn't happen to see that gal, did ya?"

"I did. We talked."

"Is she any good?"

"She is an excellent hunter."

"For a woman?"

"For anyone."

"Why not take her out there to help you?"

"I hunt alone."

"Yeah, you said that before."

"Thank you for your time, Sheriff."

"That's my job," Dekker said, "to give folks my time."

As the Cree turned to leave, Dekker spoke. "Hey, Fiddler?"

"Yes?"

"When you say you don't want amateurs out there shootin' at each other, and you, that include me?"

Fiddler just stared at the sheriff for a few moments, then turned and left the office.

SEVEN

Dakota gingerly lifted one foot and set it in the tub. The water was hot, and it took a few moments before the other foot followed. Once she was in the tub, she lowered her big butt into the water until she was finally sitting down.

She hadn't had a bath in a month of Sundays and she had to admit the hot water felt good on her skin. She grabbed the soap and began to lather herself up, and as she did her thoughts drifted to Clint Adams. What was it about the man that every time he looked at her she tingled between her legs? She hadn't been with a man in a while, maybe that was it. In fact, she was thirty-six and hadn't been with many men in her life. Toby Mathers had popped her cherry when she was fourteen, and they'd done it every Saturday for a couple of months after that. But when his folks moved him away, she didn't do it with anybody else for a couple of years, and then there was her uncle when she was sixteen. He did her in the barn a couple of times a week for about a month before he moved on. She liked it well enough, but she doubted either one of them had her liking in mind. They pretty much rutted away until they were done, and then he rolled off her.

In fact, that was pretty much her experience with men from that point on. Never really met one who didn't fuck like his ass was on fire and he had to get out of there.

She wondered if Clint Adams would be any different. While she thought about him, she soaped her legs, her thighs, and then, oh Lord, she was soaping her twitchit kinda hard, getting it nice and clean and tingly until suddenly she spasmed and had to grab both sides of the tub for support.

When she caught her breath, she thought that was the most pleasure she'd ever had with a man, let alone from just thinking about one.

After Dakota left, Clint went back to the bar and got himself a fresh beer. There were some poker games starting around the room, but he'd had too many beers to take part in them. He hated to gamble when he was drunk.

"Who—or what—the hell was that?" the bartender asked.

"That was a woman."

"Really? You couldn't tell by me."

"Oh, I think there was a woman there, all right, under all the dirt."

"What about the smell?"

"That'll come off in the bath, like the dirt," Clint said. "You'll see."

"You convinced her to take a bath?"

"I'm a very persuasive man."

"You must be."

"For instance," he went on, "I'm going to convince you to give me a beer on the house."

The bartender grinned and said, "Coming up."

In another corner of the saloon three men sat and watched Clint Adams at the bar.

"You sure that's the Gunsmith?" Eddie Largent asked.

"Big as life," Denny Blaine said. "I seen him in Denver, once."

"What was you doin' in Denver?" Pat Sanchez asked.

"I was screwin' your Mexican mama," Blaine said. "What the hell does it matter what I was doin' there? I seen him!"

"Think he's here for the bounty?" Largent asked.

"I ain't never heard of him chasin' no bounty," Blaine said, "but things change."

"What chance we got if'n he's gonna be huntin'?" Sanchez asked.

"Shut up, Pat," Blaine said.

"Why you always tellin' me to shut up?"

"Because you're always askin' stupid questions, that's why," Largent said.

Sanchez thought about protesting, but decided to pout instead.

"Bad enough we got that old Indian in town," Largent said.

"That Fiddler," Blaine said. "Some day soon he's just gonna fall off his horse and die."

"What about Dakota?"

"Her?" Blaine snorted. "She's held together by dirt and stink. She won't be a problem."

"So then the only problem will be this Wen-digo, or whatever it is," Sanchez said.

"I'm tellin' ya," Blaine said to both men, "it's a goddamned bear. It's gotta be."

"And we can kill a bear," Sanchez said.

"Yeah," Blaine said, "we can, and collect the five-hundred-dollar bounty."

"We gonna split that even?" Sanchez asked.

"We sure are, Pat," Blaine said. "Two hundred for me and Denny and a whole hundred for you."

Pat Sanchez's eyes glittered and he said, "Hot damn!"

Using the mirror behind the bar, Clint could watch the three men who had been studying him. It was his guess they were either after him for his rep, or they were hunters looking at him as competition. That five-hundred-dollar bounty was bringing them into town, and because it wasn't a huge amount of money, it was going to bring in quite a few penny-ante hunters. If it were, say, twenty-five hundred dollars, then the professional hunters would be coming in. So far, the only pros he'd seen or heard about were Dakota and Fiddler, and they were here because they were from these parts—meaning Northern Minnesota and the southern part of Canada.

And, of course, it was more than money that had brought Jack Fiddler. From what Clint had heard, this man considered hunting Wendigos as his mission in life. The bounty—or his fee, whatever he could work out—was just to keep him going.

He finally decided that the three men were hunters. They didn't have the look of hard cases who'd be out to prove their mettle against the Gunsmith.

He turned his thoughts to Dakota.

EIGHT

Clint was thinking about calling it a night—he'd had enough beer, and poker was still not a draw—when the batwings opened and a woman stepped in. He didn't recognize her at first, but then he did, from the way her body looked and the way she moved. Her face and hair, though, looked as if they belonged to somebody else entirely.

"Don't tell me . . ." the bartender said, coming over to Clint.

"I told you there was a woman underneath that dirt," Clint said.

"You was right, friend."

Dakota saw Clint at the bar and came walking over. Apparently, she'd had some clean clothes in her gear, and she seemed very uncomfortable in them. She'd left the bandolier behind, but was still wearing her gun.

"I feel funny," she said when she reached him.

"You look great," he said. "Your hair's beautiful."

She touched it quickly and said, “It is?”

“And it smells clean.”

“That’s just the soap,” she said, smelling her own hand and arm. “I think I used too much.”

“You can’t use too much soap, Dakota,” Clint told her.

“Well, I still feel funny.”

“Would you like a beer?”

“Yeah, I would.”

Clint signaled the bartender. He brought one over and gave Dakota a long look before drawing back.

“What’s his problem?”

“Don’t think he’s seen a pretty woman around here in a long time.”

She looked at him as if he was crazy.

“You think I’m pretty?”

“I think you’re very pretty.”

She blushed, and it embarrassed her and made her mad.

“Cut it out,” she said. She took a big swallow of her beer. “Okay, so I took a bath. Now you got to hold up your end of the bargain.”

“I’ll talk to the sheriff about getting you in to talk to the mayor,” he said.

“That ain’t what you said,” she told him. “You said you’d come talk to the mayor with me.”

“Is that what I said?”

“I wouldn’ta taken a bath, otherwise.”

“Okay, okay,” he said. “Don’t get upset. I’ll do my best to get the mayor to see us tomorrow.”

“Okay.”

A couple of cowboys walked past, looked Dakota up and down.

"What are ya lookin' at?" she demanded.

Both men quickened their pace and went out, the batwings swinging hard behind them.

"Take it easy," Clint said. "You scrubbed the dirt off and now men are noticing what an attractive woman you are."

"Stop sayin' stuff like that!"

"Why?"'

"I ain't used ta it." She sulked. "I don't know what to do."

"When somebody compliments you," Clint said, "it's usually polite to say thank you. That's all."

"I ain't used ta bein' polite."

"Well, nobody says you have to get used to it," Clint said. "If you don't want to do it, don't do it."

"Really?"

"Really," he said. "Also, the nice thing about a bath is that it doesn't last very long. Once you step outside, you start getting dirty again."

She stared at him steadily for a moment, then asked, "Are you makin' fun of me?"

"Maybe," he said, then added, "just a little."

"Who the heck is that?" Pat Sanchez asked when Dakota joined Clint at the bar.

The two men with him turned their heads to have a look.

"I don't believe it," Denny Blaine said.

"Is that Dakota?" Largent asked.

"It sure is."

"I ain't never seen her look like that."

"That's because you ain't never seen her so clean," Blaine said. "I wonder what made her clean up?"

"Maybe it was the Gunsmith," Sanchez said.

"Shut up, Pat," Blaine said. "She must have somethin' up her sleeve."

"You mean she's pullin' somethin'?" Largent asked.

"Yeah," Blaine said, "that's the only reason she'd take a bath and wear clean clothes."

"I wonder what it is?"

Pat Sanchez was going to take a guess. But he knew they'd just tell him to shut up again, so he kept quiet.

NINE

"What if they're teamin' up?" Largent asked.

"Whataya mean?" Blaine asked.

"Adams and Dakota," Largent said. "What if they team up and hunt this . . . thing together? Then we gotta worry about Jack Fiddler *and* them."

Blaine rubbed his jaw.

"You might have a point."

"So what do we do about it?"

"I know what I'd do," Pat Sanchez said.

Blaine looked at him and asked, "What? What would you do, Pat?"

"I'd get rid of them two."

"And how would you do that, Pat?" Largent asked.

"I'd kill 'em both."

"Dakota and the Gunsmith?" Blaine was surprised.

"I ain't afraid of no Gunsmith," Sanchez said, puffing up his chest.

Blaine and Largent both studied Sanchez. He was twenty-three, ten years younger than both of them. He was young, and he was annoying.

"So why not?"

"Okay," Blaine said, as Largent nodded to him. "Show us."

"What?"

"Show us how you'd do it."

"Well . . . I'd wait for them outside and take them when they wuz walkin' to the hotel."

"He didn't say *tell us*," Largent pointed out. "He said *show us*."

"Ya mean . . . go do it?"

"Unless you've scared," Largent said.

"I tol' ya I ain't scared."

"Then like I said," Blaine told him, "show us."

Sanchez glared at both of them, then said, "Fine, I will show you. Both of you."

He got up and stormed out of the saloon.

"You think he'll really do it?" Largent asked.

"Naw, he ain't that dumb."

"What if he is?" Largent asked. "He might get killed."

"Yeah, maybe," Blaine said, "and maybe he'll take one of them with him. Either way we make out. And if he gets killed, we get more of a split."

"I didn't think of that," Largent said.

Blaine sat back and said, "I did."

Dakota had a few more beers while Clint nursed the same one, and before long she was drunk.

"Come on," he said at one point, "I'll get you back to your hotel."

"Why?" she asked. "Ain't there no more men here that wanna compliment me?"

"There probably are," he said, "but I think you need to get some rest. You've got a big day ahead of you."

"Oh, I get it." She poked him in the chest with her forefinger. "You want me all to yourself."

"Now you've got it," he said. "Come on, I'll keep you all to myself at the hotel."

He took her by the shoulders, turned her, and propelled her toward the doors.

Outside a nervous Pat Sanchez found himself a spot in a doorway across from the saloon. He figured when Clint Adams and Dakota came out, he'd follow them. He didn't know if they were staying at the same hotel or not, but it didn't matter. As long as they were walking together, he'd get them—both of them. Two bullets—one each in the back—and he'd show Blaine and Largent who was scared and who wasn't.

See if they told him to shut up after that.

Outside Clint had to hold onto Dakota to keep her walking in a straight line, and she didn't seem to mind. He didn't, either. Holding her confirmed what he'd thought: She had a solid body, heavy breasts, and good thighs—a big girl in every way, but not at all fat. She smelled good, too, and he took advantage of that, leaning in to sniff her hair. He knew the condition wouldn't last long.

"Hey, what're ya doin'?" she asked, leaning away.

"Just smelling you."

"Oh, yeah?" she leaned back in. "How about I smell you. How would you like that?"

"I'd like that fine."

"Oh, yeah? Next thing I know you'll be wantin' ta kiss me."

"When was the last time you were kissed, Dakota?"

"Loonng time," she said, thought about it, then nodded and said again, "Long time."

He turned her to face him and would have kissed her, but that was when the shooting started.

TEN

Clint grabbed Dakota and took her down to the ground. He was surprised to find her gun in her hand by the time they hit the dirt. It impressed him. Even drunk, she thought to go for her gun.

He didn't know where the shots had come from, but when a third was fired and he saw the muzzle flash, he fired at it twice. Dakota saw where he was shooting and did the same.

They heard glass break, but at least one chunk of lead must have hit home. Someone cried out, and then a man came staggering out of the darkness, gun dangling from his hand, into the center of the street, where he went sprawling face first.

Clint and Dakota came up off the ground and walked over to where the man was lying. His gun was in the dirt next to him and Clint kicked it away. He then leaned over and turned the man over onto his back. He was young, early twenties, and Clint thought he had seen him before.

"Know him?" he asked Dakota.

"No," she said. "Never saw him before. You?"

"I think so . . . I don't know him, but I'm pretty sure I've seen him."

They both looked up as they heard footsteps approaching. Some of the men came running from the saloon, but in front of the pack was Sheriff Dekker.

"What the hell's goin' on?" he demanded.

"Damned if we know, Sheriff," Clint said. "We were just walking back to the hotel when this jasper opened fire on us from behind."

"You kill him?" Dekker asked.

"We both returned fire, Sheriff," Dakota said. "No way of knowing which one of us killed him."

"Know 'im?"

"No," she said.

"I've seen him before," Clint said, "since I came to town, but I don't know where."

"Anybody know this kid?" Dekker asked the group of men behind him.

Some men stepped forward to look and shook their heads. The others just stayed where they were.

"Okay, Lenny, you and Zeke and a couple of others carry him over to the undertaker. I'll check his pockets there." He turned to Clint, who had replaced the spent shells in his gun and was holstering it. "Where were you goin'?"

"Back to the hotel."

"You both stayin' at the same one?"

"Yes."

"Go, then," Dekker said. "I'll talk to both of you tomorrow. The rest of ya get goin'. Ain't nothin' ta see here."

"Sheriff?" Clint said.

"Yeah?"

"We're both fine, thanks for asking."

Clint took Dakota's arm, turned her, and they headed for the hotel.

As the men started to file back in to the saloon, Denny Blaine reached out and grabbed one by the arm. He and Largent had not left their table.

"What happened out there?"

"Some fella tried to back-shoot the Gunsmith and the woman he was with," the man said.

"How did he do?"

"He's dead."

"Too bad," Blaine said, releasing the man's arm.

"Told you he'd get himself killed," Largent said.

"Yup. You want another beer?"

"Well," Dakota said, "nothin' like gettin' shot at to sober a girl up, huh?"

"Or a man, for that matter," Clint said. They had entered the hotel lobby and were walking to the stairs. "You did really well, by the way."

"Thanks," she said. "That's a big compliment comin' from you."

"And you thanked me for it," Clint said. "See? You're learning."

When they got to the second floor, he walked her to her door. They stopped there.

"Well . . ." she said.

"I'll talk to the sheriff in the morning about getting to see the mayor," he said. "I'll keep my word."

"I figured you would."

"Would you like to have breakfast together in the morning?" he asked.

"I'd like that," she said.

"In the lobby at eight?" he asked.

"Sounds good."

"Well," he said, "I'm just down the hall. Good night."

"Good night."

As he walked to his door, she put the key in hers, unlocked it, opened it, and went inside.

ELEVEN

Clint got as far as taking off his gun belt when there was a knock on his door. He removed the gun from the holster, dropping the belt on the bed, and went to the door.

"Who is it?"

"Dakota."

He opened the door, holding the gun in plain sight. She stood in the hall, hands clasped in front of her, looking a lot younger than her thirty-six years. She had not removed any of her clothes or her gun belt.

"Is something wrong?" he asked.

"Yes," she said. "Can I come in?"

"Sure."

He backed away to let her enter, then took a quick look in the hall before closing the door and turning to face her.

"What's wrong?"

"You were about to do something in the street

before the shooting started," she said. "Do you remember?"

"I remember."

"Well . . . it's still been a long time for me," she said. "Do you think you could do it . . . now?"

Sheriff Dekker finished going through the dead man's pockets and came up empty.

"Albert, you didn't take anythin' off him, did you?" he asked the undertaker.

"That's a insult, Sheriff," the man said.

"Albert . . ."

The old man rubbed his hands together, making a dry, raspy sound, and said, "I did take a few dollars from him. Ya know, ta pay for the burial."

"I don't care about the money, Albert," Dekker said. "I'm lookin' for somethin' that'll tell me who he is or where he's from. All I know is that he's a stranger in town."

"Well, I ain't taken anythin' like that, Sheriff."

"You sure you didn't take, say, a letter so you could write to the family and ask for more money?"

"I swear, Sheriff," the man said. "I didn't take nothin' but a few—mebbe five dollars."

"Well," Dekker said, "he musta been sittin' with somebody in the saloon. All right, Albert. I'm done."

Albert walked the sheriff to the door, locked it when the lawman stepped outside. Dekker figured no one was going to admit to sitting with the man, not after he'd tried to back-shoot the Gunsmith. He decided to save his questions for the bartender until the morning, then went home to get some sleep. Tomorrow there would likely be more hunters—most of them amateurs—coming to town in response to the bounty.

Wait until they found the mayor was raising it.

Jack Fiddler heard the shooting from his camp, but didn't bother going to see what was going on. It wasn't any of his business. His business was the Wendigo, and that was all he was concerned with. He pulled his blanket around him and moved closer to the fire. That old horse of his would warn him if anybody came close to camp. He was asleep in seconds.

Clint picked up the holster from the bed, slid the gun home, and hung the belt on the bedpost. Then he turned to Dakota, who was waiting for an answer. He walked to her, took her in his arms, and kissed her deeply, lovingly—and longer than he'd intended, because it was so good he didn't want it to end. Her mouth came alive, as did her tongue, and she writhed against him as if trying to get closer and closer to him.

"Oh, God," she said when they broke the kiss.

"Was it the way you remembered?" he asked, not releasing his hold on her. He could feel her full breasts pressing against him, and the heat from her crotch was driving right through the double-layer denim that was between them.

"No," she said breathlessly, "I ain't never been kissed like that, Clint."

"Well, maybe you would be if you'd let men see what you really look like, Dakota."

"I've been with men before," she said. "They never seemed real worried about what I felt. They was always worried about their own feelings."

"Then you haven't been with any real men," he said, toying with the top button of her shirt. "A real man makes sure the woman he's with is happy before he worries about his own pleasure."

"I don't think so," she said. "I mean—I don't think there's any other men like you out there. Can we, uh, kiss some more?"

"As much as you want."

"I mean . . . it felt good to you, too?"

"Oh, yeah," he said, touching her lower lip with his thumb, "it felt real good, Dakota."

He kissed her again, drawing her in as close as he could, sliding his hands down to the small of her back. He wanted to grab her butt with both hands and grind himself against her, but he didn't know how she would react to that.

They were both breathless this time and she stepped back to get her breath back.

"Um, I guess I should be gettin' back to my own room."

"I guess so."

"Not that I really want ta go," she said. "If you think it's been a long time since I been kissed, it's been even longer since I been with a man.

"Dakota," he said, "I'd really like it if you stayed, but I don't want to take advantage—"

"Oh, you ain't," she said hurriedly. "I'm as sober as a judge, I swear. Know what I'm doin'."

"Well, then, I guess the first thing you should do is take off that gun belt."

TWELVE

"Where are we goin'?" Largent asked Blaine.

"We're gettin' out of here before the law comes askin' questions."

"About what?" Largent asked. He was still seated while Blaine was standing. "We didn't do nothin'."

"Look, Eddie, we don't wanna be sittin' here when the law comes in askin' questions about Sanchez."

"All we gotta say is we didn't know 'im."

"And what if somebody tells the sheriff he was sittin' with us?" Blaine asked.

Largent chewed his lower lip.

"I didn't think about that."

"Well, that's why I do the thinkin'," Blaine said. "So get yer ass up and let's get over to the rooming house. We gotta get some sleep, anyway."

Largent stood and asked. "We gonna start huntin' that thing tomorrow?"

"Bright and early, son," Blaine said, "bright and early."

• • •

Clint undressed Dakota gingerly. First her shirt, then her trousers, and then he discovered that she didn't wear any frilly undergarments. She had on a pair of long johns.

"Guess this looks kinda funny, huh?" she asked, standing there in her long underwear.

"If you saw what I see, you wouldn't think it was funny. You'd think it was . . . kinda sexy."

He could see the size and shape of her big, pear-shaped breasts right through the flannel, and the big nipples that were poking against it. He walked up to her and cupped her breasts right through the fabric, grazed the nipples with his thumbs and then kissed her again. This time, while he kissed her, he undid the long underwear, and then started peeling it off her. When he had it down to her waist, he stepped back and stared at her pale, goose-dappled flesh, and her pink nipples.

"You're beautiful," he said.

"I ain't."

"Yeah, you are. Let's get this all the way off."

He pulled the underwear down to her ankles, and then she stepped out of them. He tossed them away and took another look. The patch of hair between her legs was even paler than the hair on her head, and it was unruly. He stepped closer and ran his hands over her body, cupping the breasts again, sliding them around to touch her buttocks and then her thighs. He put one hand between them, cupped her crotch, and used his thumb to probe into the hair. He found her wet and slick, and she caught her breath as he stroked her.

"Oh, Jesus," she said, "my legs are weak."

He guided her to the bed, sat her down, and began to undress.

"I ain't never watched a man undress before," she said.

"Well, it ain't much to see," he said. When he stepped out of his clothes and stood before her naked, his erection was at full attention.

She reached out for him, pulled back, then reached again. This time she took his pole in her hand and stroked it, examined it. She reached beneath him to cup his balls, and then stroke them.

"Lie back," he said. He didn't think she'd be ready for any playing around. He knew he wasn't. He wanted to be inside her.

She lay back on the bed and she was a sight to behold. The light from the lamp made her hair—both on her head and between her legs—almost glow. It even picked up the light hairs on her forearms. Her arms seemed to glow, as well.

He got in bed with her, spread her legs, positioned himself between her thighs, and pressed the big, spongy head of his dick to her moist slit. She gasped, and opened her legs even wider for him. He slid into her nice and slow, but all the way in so that she bit her lip as her eyes widened. She was steamy and wet. He began to move in and out of her, propping himself up on his arms, looking down on her face. As he fucked her, he leaned down and kissed her mouth, sliding his tongue in and out, and then moved down to lick and bite her big nipples.

"Oh, God, Clint," she said, "I ain't never had it like this."

He put his mouth to her ear, which only served to excite her more, and said, "This is just the beginning."

"Don't know if I can take any more."

"Don't worry," he said, "you will."

He lowered his weight onto her. She was big and strong enough to take it. He slid his hands beneath her, cupped her big buttocks, and began to fuck her faster, going as deep as he could each time, squeezing her ass, pulling her to him. Her arms and legs went around him and she found his tempo and began moving along with him. Before long they were both mindless as their flesh slapped together, and their passions rose . . .

THIRTEEN

By morning Dakota had lost all sense of shyness. She woke him by taking his cock in her mouth and sucking it until it was erect, then sliding up and sitting on top of him, taking him deep inside her. She rode him that way, her head tossed back, her hands pressed down onto his abdomen. He reached up and took hold of her breasts, cupping them so they wouldn't bounce so much and so he could suck and lick her nipples some more.

"Oh, God, oh, God, oh, God," she moaned as she bounced up and down on him.

He started to feel his orgasm rising up inside of him so he forcefully flipped her over, took hold of her ankles, held her legs apart, and fucked her that way until he exploded inside of her. After a full night of seeing to her needs, he didn't think she'd mind if he saw to his own pleasure just once . . .

Since they had planned on having breakfast together anyway, they stuck to that plan. It was the first such meal for either of them in town, so they walked a ways until they found a small café and then went inside. It seemed like they'd made a good choice, because the place was crowded. Clint wasn't able to get a table in a corner, but they did get one that was away from the windows.

"I'll watch your back," she promised him.

After the way she had reacted to the shooting the night before, he had no doubt that she was capable of doing that.

Once they ordered their breakfast, she asked, "Which one of us do you think killed him last night?"

"Does it matter?"

"Well . . . I was kinda hopin' it wasn't me," she said. "Is that terrible?"

"No, not at all," he said.

"See, I don't make a habit of killin' people," she said. "I hunt animals."

"Have you ever killed anyone?" he asked, because she'd been vague about it.

"Seems I'm admittin' to you all the things I ain't done—or ain't done in a long time—but no, I never shot a man before."

"Well, to tell you the truth," he said, "as quickly as you acted, I think I managed to get off two shots first. I'm pretty sure I got him, and he only had one hole in him."

"Thanks for that," she said. "Guess we're gonna have to talk to the sheriff sooner or later."

"Looks like sooner," he told her. "He just walked in."

Sheriff Dekker crossed the room and approached their table.

"You folks mind if I join ya?" he asked.

"Have a seat, Sheriff," Clint said. "Full breakfast or just coffee?"

"Coffee," he said, pulling a chair out and sitting. "I had my breakfast already. Good morning, Miss Dakota."

"It's just Dakota, Sheriff," she said. "Nobody calls me Miss."

"Pardon me, ma'am," he said, "but a lady as pretty as you deserves some respect—if you don't mind me sayin' so."

"No, Sheriff," she said, "I don't mind at all."

"Any word on who that young fellow I shot is, Sheriff?" Clint asked.

"Nothin'," Dekker said. "Had nothin' on him that would identify him, and the bartender didn't know who he was. Did say he thought he saw him sittin' with some fellers in the saloon."

Clint snapped his fingers.

"That's where I saw him," he said. "There were three of them sitting together, and they seemed real interested in me."

"I wonder why all three wouldn't have tried for you, then?" Dekker asked. "They might have had a better chance."

"Well, from what I saw of Dakota out there I think she and I could have handled them," Clint said, "but apparently they sent their youngest and least experienced hand after us."

"Us?" Dekker asked.

"Us?" Dakota echoed.

"Well," Clint said, "of course, we're assuming they were after me, but . . ."

"Why would they be after Dakota?" Dekker asked.

"Yeah," she said, "why me?"

"I didn't say they were. I just said we don't know for sure who the kid was shooting at."

"I don't like the sound of that," Dakota said. "I ain't done nothin' to nobody to make them wanna kill me."

"Well, there is a bounty on the head of the Wendigo," Clint said. "Maybe they thought with you out of the way they'd have a better chance."

"Well, they'd better worry a little bit more about Jack Fiddler," she said.

"That's a good point," Clint said. "Dakota, do you know where he's camped?"

"Yeah, he told me last night."

"Maybe after breakfast we'd better go and pay him a visit, see if he had any adventures during the night."

"Good idea," Dekker said. "Let me know what you find out."

The waiter came with their breakfasts. Dekker decided to forgo the coffee and leave them to it.

FOURTEEN

Dakota told Clint where Jack Fiddler's camp was supposed to be. After breakfast they simply walked north of town until they came to it. Actually, they smelled the camp before they saw it. Coffee and beans.

As they entered the camp, Fiddler looked up at Dakota.

"I been waitin' for you," he said. "Who's your friend?"

"Jack, this is Clint Adams."

Fiddler looked at Clint. The Indian did look ancient, he had to admit.

"Why is the Gunsmith huntin' the Wendigo?"

"He isn't," Clint said. "I'm just passing through. I didn't want to pass up the chance to meet Jack Fiddler."

"You know me?"

"I've heard of you."

"Hunker down," he told them. "Drink coffee with me."

They did as he asked and he passed them each a full cup. Clint tasted it.

"This is damn good," he said. "I thought Indians didn't like coffee."

"They don't," Fiddler said. "I do."

"Well, you make it damn good, too."

Fiddler smiled, revealing more gaps than yellowed teeth.

"Somebody took a couple of shots at us last night, Jack," Dakota said.

"I heard the shots. Sorry it was you. You killed him?"

"I did."

"I might have," she said. "But it's more likely Clint's shot got him."

"Good," Fiddler said. "Hunters like you and me, we don't kill men."

"No, we don't," Dakota said.

"Which one of you was he after?"

"We're not sure," Clint said. "Most likely me, but if it was hunters looking to whittle at the competition, they might make a try at you. Did you hear anyone near your camp last night?"

"No."

"Did you sleep?" Clint asked.

'Yes, but Horse would have warned me."

"Horse?" Clint asked. "The mare's name is Horse?"

Fiddler shrugged.

"Well," Clint said, handing back the empty cup, "I just wanted to warn you."

"Thank you."

"You two probably want to talk."

"You want another cup?"

"Sure," Clint said.

Fiddler poured and handed it to him, then warmed up Dakota's and his own.

"When are you goin' out, Jack?" Dakota asked.

"This mornin'," Fiddler said. "I have to pick up my supplies, my packhorse, and then I'll start. Want to help an old man?" he asked Dakota.

"Like you need help."

"You could pick up my supplies for me," he said, "while I pick up the horse. Then I can get started sooner."

"Sure, Fiddler," Dakota said. "I'll help you."

Fiddler looked at Clint.

"Are you stayin' in town?"

"For a day or two," Clint said. "I may not want to hunt the Wendigo, but I'd like to be around when you get him." He looked at Dakota. "Or you."

"You're supposed to get me in to see the mayor." Dakota reminded Clint.

"Oh, yeah," Clint said. "I should get on that while you help Fiddler."

They all finished their coffee and stood up.

"I'll put out the fire and meet you back here," Fiddler told Dakota.

"Fine." She turned to Clint. "Where should I meet you after you talk to the sheriff?"

"How about the hotel?"

"Good. I'll see you there in . . . an hour?" She looked at the old Cree hunter.

"I will not need you for more than an hour," Fiddler confirmed.

"All right, then," Clint said. "At the hotel in an hour. Good luck with your hunt, Fiddler."

Fiddler pointed a crooked index finger at Clint.

"You are truly not here to hunt the Wendigo?"

"Fiddler," Clint said, "I am truly not here to hunt anyone or anything . . . especially not the Wendigo."

Fiddler studied Clint for a long moment, then lowered his finger and said, "We will see."

FIFTEEN

Clint found Sheriff Dekker in his office. The man was surprised to see Clint so soon.

"What brings you back here?"

"Dakota and I checked on Jack Fiddler," Clint said. "He spent an uneventful night."

"Well, that's good."

"I have another matter to talk to you about, though."

"What's that?"

"Dakota would like to talk to the mayor."

"What for?"

"To make a case for herself being hired by the town to hunt the Wendigo."

"The town hired Fiddler," Dekker said. "In fact, she's better off going for the bounty. We're upping it today to a thousand dollars."

"A thousand is just going to bring more amateurs to town," Clint warned.

"I know that," Dekker said, spreading his hands. "It's not my decision to make."

"Well, I promised Dakota I'd try to get her in to see the mayor," Clint said. "I tried."

"Wait," Dekker said as Clint headed for the door.

"What?"

"You've gotten pretty friendly with Dakota already, haven't you?" Dekker asked.

"What's that mean?"

"Hey, no offense," Dekker said, holding his hands out. "All I meant was, the mayor would agree to see her if it included you."

Clint turned to face the lawman.

"Okay, yeah, I did say I'd go with her."

"Great," Dekker said. "I'll set it up. How about noon?"

"That's fine," Clint said. "Thanks."

As Clint started to leave, Dekker stood up to intensify his point.

"He'll agree to hire you," he said. "Even though Fiddler's already on the payroll."

"He won't hire three people, though, will he?"

"Maybe not," Sheriff Dekker said, "but I bet he'd hire two partners."

"Partners."

"Think it over."

"Yeah," Clint said unhappily, "I will."

He left the office, already knowing he'd gotten himself roped into something . . . again.

Dakota was waiting for him in the lobby when he got to the hotel.

"Did you talk to the mayor?" she asked.

"I talked to the sheriff, who said the mayor will see us at noon," he replied.

"Us? So you'll go with me?"

"Yes, I will."

She looked like she was going to hug him, but drew back at the last minute. She'd lost some of her inhibitions in his room the night before, but they were still very much in evidence in the hotel lobby.

"That's great. What do we do until then?"

"What you'd normally do before you go hunting," Clint said. "What would that be?"

"I'd clean my guns, make sure they're workin' the way they're supposed to. I don't wanna come face to face with a Wendigo only to have my gun misfire."

"Well, then, get to it," he said.

"What about you?"

"I can keep myself busy."

She smiled and said, "We could keep each other busy."

"That wouldn't get your guns clean, would it?"

She stuck her tongue out at him and said, "I'll meet you down here at two o'clock. We can have a drink before we go and see the mayor."

"One drink," Clint cautioned. "You don't want to be drunk when you're pleading your case."

"Or our case."

"What do you mean?"

"What if we went in as . . . partners?"

Just for a moment he wondered if she'd somehow been listening to his conversation with the sheriff.

"You wouldn't mind that?"

"I think together we'd be the perfect hunter," she said. "Maybe better than Fiddler. My hunting skills and your ability with guns. We'd be unbeatable."

"I didn't know it was a contest."

"When there's money involved, it's always a contest."

"Why don't we see how receptive the mayor is, first?"

She smiled and said, "Deal."

SIXTEEN

After leaving Dakota, Clint went back to Jack Fiddler's camp, hoping to catch the old Cree before he left for his hunt. Luckily, the man was still loading his packhorse with supplies.

Clint entered the camp, knowing that Fiddler was aware of him there.

"You are back with somethin' on your mind," Fiddler said.

"How do you know?"

"You have returned without Dakota," Fiddler said. "So this must be about her."

"It is."

Fiddler turned to face Clint.

"Can you convince her not to hunt the Wendigo?"

"I doubt it."

"So then you will go with her."

"But I told you I would not hunt," Clint pointed out.

Fiddler waved that away.

"I do not want her to be hurt," he said. "With you along there is less chance of that."

"So you don't mind?"

"You came seekin' my permission?" the Cree hunter asked.

"Not permission as much as . . . dispensation."

"You have it," Fiddler said.

"Thank you."

"What else?"

"Is there something else?"

"Is there?"

Clint hesitated.

"You want to know about the Wendigo," the Cree said.

"Yes."

"You do not believe."

"It's not that, but . . ."

"I have seen them," Fiddler said. "I have seen what they have done. And I have killed them."

"How?"

"With magic."

"Not guns?"

"Not your guns," Fiddler said. "Not Dakota's. To hunt the Wendigo with only guns is foolhardy."

"So everyone else who hunts them is . . . suicidal?"

"As I said," Fiddler corrected. "Foolhardy. Each does it for his or her own reason."

"I think most of them are going to be doing it for the thousand dollars."

"Thousand?"

"It goes up today."

Fiddler just shook his head.

"I must go," he said. "The sooner I kill it, the more lives will be spared."

"Can't you give me any advice, Fiddler?" Clint asked. "I'm not after the money."

"I know, my friend," Fiddler said. "You are doin' it for the woman."

"I'm doing it in the hopes of keeping the woman alive," Clint said.

"Then take the advice I give you, and take it to heart," Fiddler said.

"I will."

"Keep her away," Fiddler said. "Do not let her hunt, for the Wendigo will surely kill her—and you."

"That's it?"

"That," Jack Fiddler said, again showing Clint that crooked index finger, "is the best advice I can give you."

"Then I'll try to take it to heart."

Fiddler nodded, then shook his head as if he were thinking. "I know you will, but I also know you will not do what I say."

SEVENTEEN

When Clint met Dakota in the hotel lobby, they walked over to the saloon together and ordered a beer each.

"Before we go see the mayor, I have to talk to you about something."

"What?"

"What would you think of not hunting the Wendigo?"

"Why would I do that?"

"To stay alive."

"I'm not afraid, Clint."

"I know you're not."

"Then why would I not go?"

"I had a talk with Fiddler this morning," he admitted. "He seems to think he's the only one who can kill it."

"My bullets are as good as his."

"He says you need more than bullets," Clint replied. "You need magic."

"Clint," Dakota said, "you can't believe everything Jack Fiddler tells you. He'd old."

"No way I can talk you out of this?"

"I don't think so. There's always the money to think about."

"Oh, yeah, the money." He told her what the sheriff had said, that she might be better off going for the bounty.

"Well, like you said," she answered, "let's see what the mayor has to say."

"Okay," he said, "have it your way."

She touched his arm.

"I know you're not scared for yourself, so you're scared for me. That's nice, but I'm gonna do this—with or without you."

"I get it," he said. "Let's go see Hizzoner."

Sheriff Dekker was waiting in front of City Hall.

"Adams, Dakota," he said. "The mayor's waitin'."

"Let's go," Dakota said.

They followed the lawman into the building and to the mayor's office.

"Mayor Payne, this is Clint Adams, this is Dakota." Dekker gestured.

"Adams, this is a pleasure." The mayor, a big, florid-faced man, extended his hand and Clint shook it. "Miss Dakota."

"Just Dakota."

"I must say," he commented, "you're not quite what I expected."

"Oh," Dakota said. "Well, Clint made me take a bath."

"I see." The mayor wasn't quite sure if that was a joke or not. "Please, both of you sit."

They each took a chair. The sheriff stood in a corner with his arms folded.

"I understand you want the town to hire you to hunt this . . . this Wendigo thing."

"Well—"

"Clint and I think that together we can kill it faster than anyone else."

"Well, we certainly want this taken care of quickly," the mayor said, "but we've already hired Jack Fiddler. He has a reputation for killing these . . . things."

"Well, that's true, but Jack's . . . been at it for a while."

"Is that your way of saying he's getting old?" Payne asked Dakota.

"I'm just sayin' . . ." She trailed off and looked at Clint.

"Dakota is just saying that maybe you can use an alternative," he offered.

"Yeah," she said, "that's all I was sayin'."

"Well," Payne said, "I can tell you I wouldn't mind having the Gunsmith—and Dakota—hunting this thing."

"Then you'll do it?" Dakota asked.

"I tell you what," Payne said, "let's make a deal. If you two kill the Wendigo, we'll give you the bounty, and the town will match it. How's that? A thousand each?"

"I'm not interested in the money," Clint said. "All the money will go to Dakota."

"Whatever you want to do with the money, that's your business," Payne said. "Is it a deal?"

Clint looked at Dakota, leaving it to her.

"It's a deal, Mr. Mayor."

"The sheriff can tell you where this thing struck last," the mayor said, standing up. "I wish you both luck."

They all shook hands and then they followed Sheriff Dekker out.

"Sheriff, did Fiddler get to look at the dead man and question the survivor?" Dakota asked.

"He did it last night."

"Can we do it today?" Clint asked.

"I don't see why not?" Dekker said. "I'll take you now, and fill you in on the way."

EIGHTEEN

Two brothers had been out hunting the Wendigo after the creature had been blamed for three deaths already.

"Larry and Billy Lawrence," Dekker said. "Twenty-something, both of them. About a year apart. Fancied themselves crack shots because they could shoot jackrabbits. The boys went out a few days ago, but only Larry came back. He got me, and we went out to get his brother's body."

"How was he killed?" Clint asked.

"I'll let Larry tell you the same story he told me," Dekker said, "and Fiddler."

"First, let's see the body," Dakota said.

"It's been at the undertaker's for days," Dekker said. "Gettin' kinda ripe."

"We'll take a look at it," Clint said, "and then the undertaker can bury it."

Dekker led them to the undertaker's office.

"Albert has been the undertaker here for over twenty years," Dekker said.

"Closer to thirty," Albert said. "A pleasure to meet you, Miss Dakota. And you, Mr. Adams. You've certainly provided enough work for me and my kind over the years."

"Don't believe everything you hear, Albert."

"Well, you gave me some work yesterday."

"They're more interested in work you've still got to do, Albert," Dekker said. "They want to see Billy Lawrence's body."

"When will I be able to bury that poor boy?" Albert asked.

"Tomorrow," Dekker said, "you can bury him tomorrow. Now show them the body."

"Come with me."

"I'll wait here," Dekker said. "I've seen it too many times."

Clint and Dakota followed Albert to a room in the back. As they got closer, the smell got stronger. Clint recognized the smell of death. Dakota gagged for a moment when they reached the door. The odor didn't seem to bother the undertaker.

"Will you be all right?" Clint asked her.

"Yeah, I'll be okay," she said. "Let's go."

There was no door, only a curtain. Albert pushed it aside and they entered. The undertaker walked to a body on a table, covered by a sheet. He drew the sheet back.

"Take it off completely," Dakota said.

It was barely a body. It had been torn to shreds. An arm and a leg had been torn off and were lying on the table with it. Great chunks had been taken out of the body. If the legend of the Wendigo was true, the young man had been eaten.

"Enough?" Clint asked.

"Yeah," Dakota said.

"Cover it up," Clint said, "and get the poor bastard buried as soon as possible."

"His brother can't afford—"

"I'll pay for it," Clint said. "Give him a good coffin."

He took Dakota's arm and led her out of the room.

"I've never seen anything like that," she said when they reached Dekker.

"Neither have I," Dekker said.

"That makes three of us," Clint said. "Let's get some air."

Outside they started walking, Dekker guiding them to see the other Lawrence brother.

"Ever see a bear do that, Dakota?" Dekker asked.

"No, never."

"Do you believe in the Wendigo?" Dekker asked her.

"I never really did . . . until now."

"Clint?"

"I reserve my opinion," Clint said.

"But do you know of an animal that's ever done that?" Dekker asked. "A big cat, maybe?"

"No," Clint said. "Never."

"So then maybe old Fiddler is right," Dekker said. "There's a Wendigo, and he can kill it."

"I guess we'll find out."

Sheriff Dekker took them to a small shack outside of town to the south.

"The Lawrence boys lived here with their parents. They both died years ago. Drunks, both of them."

"How's Larry doing?" Clint asked.

"You'll see," Dekker said as they reached the door. "He's scared, won't come out of the shack for any reason. I tried—well, you'll see."

Dekker knocked, and they heard a stifled scream from inside.

NINETEEN

Dekker opened the door and the three of them went in. They found Larry Lawrence cowering on a cot. From the smell, they could tell the knock on the door had caused the man to pee his pants. They couldn't be certain because he had the sheet pulled up over him.

"Larry, it's Sheriff Dekker. It's okay. You're safe."

"Sh-sheriff?" Lawrence looked up at the man.

"I brought some people to see you," Dekker said. "Clint Adams and Dakota."

Lawrence looked up at them with frightened eyes. He had part of the sheet in his mouth.

"They're gonna kill the Wendigo for you, Larry."

Lawrence released the sheet from his mouth and said, "I thought Fiddler was gonna kill it."

"He is," Dekker said. "They're all gonna kill it. What they need from you is to tell them what you saw."

"I saw—I saw that thing kill my brother," the boy said. "He tore him apart, he . . . it ate parts of him. That's what I saw! That's what I see every time I close my eyes."

"Larry," Clint said, "what does the Wendigo look like?"

"Huge," Lawrence said, "long teeth, a head like a skull. Claws. It was horrible."

Clint looked at Dakota, who shrugged

"And yellow eyes," Lawrence said. "Don't forget it has yellow eyes. They glow in the dark!"

"Where did you and your brother—"

"I can tell you that," Dekker said. "Let's leave Larry alone now. He's got to change his trousers."

"Kill it," Larry Lawrence yelled at them from his bed. "Kill it, kill it, kill it."

"They'll kill it, Larry," Dekker said. "You change your trousers, huh?"

They could still hear him shouting "Kill it!" when they got outside.

Blaine and Largent were mounting their horses in front of the livery stable.

"So what about Fiddler?" Largent asked. "And Adams and the girl?"

"Who knows?" Blaine said. "There's gonna be a lot of amateurs out there. Who knows how many of them will shoot at anything that moves?"

Largent laughed and the two rode out of town to begin their hunt.

Clint and Dakota walked back to the sheriff's office with Dekker.

"They were in a canyon about twenty miles out of town, due north," the lawman said. "Larry said the Wendigo herded them into it and then attacked. Larry was lucky to escape while the thing was killing his brother."

"How accurate do you think he is in what he says he saw?" Clint asked.

"I think he's very accurate," Dekker said. "Unfortunately, I think he's been describing what he sees in his dreams. Especially that stuff about the glowing yellow eyes."

"I see."

"When will you be leavin'?"

"Now," Clint said. "We're going to saddle our horses and get going."

"Well, good luck," Dekker said. "I have to admit I don't care if you kill it or Fiddler does—as long as somebody gets the job done."

"We'll keep that in mind," Clint said. "Thanks for your help."

They turned and walked away from Sheriff Dekker.

"What about supplies?" Dakota asked.

"We'll saddle our horses and ride over to the general store," Clint said. "We'll travel light, whatever we can carry in our saddlebags. That okay with you, Dakota?"

"That's fine," she said. "All I usually need is some beef jerky and my guns."

"And some coffee," Clint said. "Let's not forget coffee."

When they had their saddlebags packed, they mounted their horses in front of the store.

"Did you believe the mayor?" she asked him.

"About what?"

"About doubling the bounty if we kill the Wendigo."

"You didn't?"

She blew air out of her mouth.

"Funny," Clint said, "I thought you believed him."

"He's a man, isn't he?" she asked.

"Then why hunt?" Clint asked.

"Because like Fiddler, it's not about the money," she said.

"Then why try to make a deal?"

"Because I know I need money to keep going," she said.

"Don't we all?"

TWENTY

As soon as they cleared town, Clint began to feel something in the air. He had hunted bears, cats, and men in the past, but never a mythical creature. Perhaps bears or cats that had grown to mythical proportions, but never what he considered to actually be a creature of myth.

And if he really believed it was only a myth, then what was he feeling? Surely there was no danger from a creature that did not exist? But something had torn apart Billy Lawrence. And Jack Fiddler claimed to have already killed Wendigos before—with bullets and magic.

"You're quiet," Dakota said.

"We're hunting," he said. "We're supposed to be quiet."

"Not really," she said. "Right now I'm only interested in what I see on the ground."

"And what's that?"

"Dismount," she said. "I'll show you."

They dismounted. Clint dropped Eclipse's reins to

the ground. Dakota secured her mount to a nearby bush. That would keep the animal from wandering off, but in case of danger, the horse would be able to pull free.

"Over here," she said. "See that?"

Clint looked at the ground.

"See what?"

"Not the hard ground," she said, "there." She pointed to some shrubs that had been tramped down. "We're in the northern hardwood forest. That chokecherry. See how much of it is mashed down?"

"Yes."

"Come over here."

She took him to some chokecherry shrubs and said, "Step on that."

He did and then stepped back.

"See how much of it you tramped down? Now compare."

He looked back at the original chokecherry she'd shown him.

"About twice as much, maybe more."

"Right," she said. "Something with a big foot stepped right there."

"That was done with one step?" he asked.

"Yes."

He stared at it.

"A bear?"

"Let me give you a lesson in bears," she said. "Around here you mostly see black bears. The can grow as large as seven feet in height, and weigh about five hundred pounds. The thing that made that footprint has to be ten feet tall."

"A bear can't grow to ten feet?"

"Maybe," she said. "I've never seen a black bear that big. A Kodiak, maybe. I've seen ten-foot Kodiaks that weigh up to fifteen hundred pounds, but you don't see them around here. They pretty much stick to Kodiak island."

"What about a grizzly?"

"They do grow larger than the other kinds of bears, but you see them mostly from the high plains to the Pacific, not up here. Also, do you know what bears eat?"

"Not people?"

"Right," she said. "They eat bark and berries—all kinds of fruit—and insects. Not people."

"Okay," Clint said, "so it's not a bear, unless it's a really strange one."

Dakota sighed.

"You've got to stop thinkin' about bears, Clint. And cats don't grow this big. They average about a hundred and sixty pounds, and they sure don't have paws this big."

"Okay," Clint said, "so I guess that leaves a Wendigo."

"Yeah," she said, "a Wendigo."

"Is it possible," he asked, "that the Wendigo is a living creature rather than some sort of magic myth?"

"I hope so," she said. "I'm hopin' for somethin' we can kill with bullets. If we need magic to kill it, we're gonna be shit out of luck."

They continued to ride, with Dakota taking the lead. She kept her head down, watching the ground for sign, so Clint kept his head up, watching their backs, watching for other animals or other hunters. He didn't want them getting accidentally shot by some amateurs.

Clint thought about the two men who had been in the saloon with the dead man. If Clint and Dakota were shot at by them, it would be no accident.

"I guess we could've just ridden out to that canyon," Dakota said after a while.

"Is that where the tracks are leading us?"

"Looks like."

"Then that's probably where Fiddler will go, too, isn't it?"

She turned in her saddle, looked at him, and said, "I guess we'll find out when we get there."

TWENTY-ONE

Fiddler reached the canyon late in the day. He'd been following the same trail Dakota picked up. He may have looked ancient, but his eyesight and tracking ability were still excellent. It was the white man whose eyes and stamina faded with age.

He camped just outside the canyon in a clearing that would give him enough warning if the Wendigo charged his fire, which it usually didn't do. He also had Horse, who would kick up a ruckus if she caught even a hint of Wendigo. If anything happened, the packhorse would be the first casualty, but that was all right. That was why he'd bought the animal.

While waiting for the coffee to be ready Fiddler thought back to the boy's body he saw at the undertaker's. He had, of course, seen the outcome of a Wendigo attack before, but nothing like with that boy. This particular beast had been frenzied, concerned more with ripping apart than with feeding. Fiddler even suspected he'd find the chunks of flesh that had been bitten or gouged out, unless another hungry predator had already found and consumed them.

Fiddler kept his supplies as simple as possible, even though he required the presence of a packhorse. He carried a lot of coffee and beans and some dried beef jerky, which would sustain him for the duration of his hunt. If anyone were to see his packhorse, they'd wonder why he even needed one, but that was one concession to age. He wanted to carry as little as he could on himself and on Horse.

He made his fire, cooked his coffee and beans, and sat down to eat with his rifle on the ground next to him. He wore a pistol tucked into his belt. He wasn't very good with it, but it would do for close-range work.

He ate slowly, chewing as well as he could with the collection of teeth scattered in his mouth. He thought about Dakota. He did not want her to find the Wendigo—or the Wendigo to find her—because he did not want her to die. She was a good hunter, but she should stick to animals.

As for Clint Adams, he was a legend in his own right, but he was out of his element here. He was also likely to get killed. And any number of the amateur hunters as well. Fiddler had to find the Wendigo, or attract it to him, as soon as possible.

He took out one piece of beef jerky after the beans were gone, poured himself another cup of coffee. Because of his teeth—or lack of them—the jerky was harder to eat, but he proceeded diligently.

• • •

Clint and Dakota made camp. She built the fire while he saw to the horses. She also started their food, but left the coffee to him at his request.

"I make very good trail coffee," he said.

"Good," she said, "because I don't."

She did a good job, though, with the bacon and beans, scraped it all off in equal portions, and handed him a plate and spoon.

"Jack Fiddler probably already made it to the canyon," she told him.

"You think he moved faster than we did? As old as he is and with a packhorse?"

"I wouldn't be surprised if he got there by magic," she said, "but yes, I think he did."

"Then maybe he'll kill it by the time we get there."

"I hope not."

"You'll forgive me if I hope so."

"Of course," she said. "We'll forgive each other, won't we?"

"Why not?"

"I know you don't want me to face the Wendigo, but it's something I have to do."

"Why?"

"Because I've faced every other kind of animal there is," Dakota said. "I've killed them all."

"So you feel the need to test yourself?"

"I don't think of it as testing," she said. "I'm just . . . pushin' myself."

Clint poured himself some more coffee after she shook her head declining more.

"I can understand that."

"You've pushed yourself?"

"When I was your age, or younger," he said, "yes. It was important to me . . . then.

"Then you understand."

"Yes, I do," he said, "but I still wish you wouldn't."

She smiled at him.

"Do you want to take the first watch? Or second?"

"I'll take the first," he said. "I'm not tired, and I'd like some more coffee."

"You really do like that stuff, don't you?" she asked. "I prefer whiskey."

"Do you have any with you?" he asked.

"No," she said, climbing into her bedroll. "I don't drink when I'm huntin'."

She turned over, put her back to the fire, and he said softly, "Neither do I."

TWENTY-TWO

Camped a few miles away were Denny Blaine and Ed Largent, sitting around a fire cooking up bacon and beans. The wind was blowing the scent of their food toward Clint and Dakota's camp, but they couldn't smell it because of their own cooking odors.

"We're ridin' around in circles," Largent complained.

"I told you," Blaine said, "I'm trackin' the thing."

"I don't see any tracks."

"That's why it's my job," Blaine said. "Just relax, Ed. The only ones out here are us, Fiddler, and Adams and the girl. Tomorrow these woods will be crawling with every idiot who thinks they can shoot a gun. We've got a head start."

"Fiddler," Largent said, "he's the one who's gonna get it—and the money."

"No," Blaine said, "we're gonna get it and the money. That's the way it's gonna be."

Largent glumly moved his food around his plate.

"You've got first watch, Ed," Blaine said. He placed his head on his saddle and promptly went to sleep.

Largent couldn't have slept if he tried, so he didn't mind taking first watch. After half an hour, Blaine was snoring noisily and Largent was pouring himself some more coffee when he heard something moving in the brush. He stood up quickly and drew his gun. He was going to shout, "Who's there?" when he suddenly wondered if Wendigo's could talk.

Something moved again, making enough of a racket that he thought Blaine should've woke up.

"Somethin's out there," Largent said.

Blaine kept snoring.

"Denny, wake up!" he said. "Somethin' comin'."

Blaine snorted, but didn't move.

"Goddamn it, Denny—" Largent snarled, but he got no further. Whatever it was in the brush suddenly came out and moved at him with incredible speed. He saw large teeth, and two burning, yellow eyes.

"Oh, my God," he breathed.

He got off two shots—and no more.

Blaine came blearily awake in time to see Ed Largent's head bouncing toward him.

"Jesus—" he cried out, scooting back so it wouldn't hit him.

And then he saw it.

"Crap!" he said.

He drew his weapon. He had time to stand up, no time to pull the trigger of his gun, but plenty of time to scream . . .

• • •

From his camp Fiddler heard the shots, and then the scream. It came from far enough away that he knew the Wendigo would not be coming for him this night. It had already fed. Even Horse was standing more quietly now.

Calmly, he rolled over, wrapped the blanket around himself, put his head on his saddle, and went to sleep.

Clint came awake as soon as the shots were fired. He rolled away from his bedroll and got to his feet. He had his gun in his hand, as did Dakota.

"Did you hear that?" Dakota asked.

"I heard it," Clint said. "It's not far."

They both stood there, listening, and then the scream came, drawn out, and then abruptly cut off.

"Jesus," she said, "it's out there. Somebody's in trouble. Come on!"

"Wait!" He grabbed her arm.

"We have to go—"

"Where?" he asked. "They're already dead, whoever the poor bastards are. What good would it do for us to go traipsing around in the dark? We'd only end up dead, too, more than likely."

"But—"

"But what, Dakota?"

She looked at him helplessly.

"They may need help."

"I think you know better than that," he said. "You heard that scream cut off."

"Jesus," she said again, shaking her head. "That poor bastard."

"I just hope it wasn't Fiddler," Clint said, sliding his gun back into his holster.

"It wasn't."

He looked at her.

"How do you know?"

"Jack Fiddler would never scream like that," she said. "Never."

TWENTY-THREE

In the morning they changed direction and rode toward the sound of the shots and the scream. If Fiddler had gotten to the canyon already, they couldn't help it. But they needed to know what had happened in the night.

When they reached the camp, there was still some smoke trailing up from the fire. In the morning sunlight they could see the blood on the ground, the bits of body strewn about, and in one spot the severed head.

"Jesus," she said.

They wanted to get closer, but Dakota's horse wouldn't budge. The smell of blood gave him a case of stiff legs.

"Let's dismount," Clint said.

They did and approached the camp, each with a gun in hand. There was a leg here and an arm there.

"How many?" she asked.

"Looks like two men," Clint said.

"Know them?"

"We have a choice," Clint said. "We can look at the head, or at that torso over there with the head still attached."

Dakota swallowed.

"You keep watch," Clint said. "I'll look at their faces."

She didn't argue.

First he leaned over so he could see the face on the head, which was in the dirt. He had to reach down with the barrel of his gun and nudge it a bit so it would turn. The eyes were still open, and the face looked familiar. When he walked over to the other one, lying on its back, he recognized them both.

"They were in the saloon last night," he said, "with the fellow who shot at us."

"And they were out here hunting," she said.

"Guess they tried to get us out of the way first," Clint said. "Little did they know they'd find the Wendigo first—or the other way around."

"This is just like the Lawrence boy," she said.

"Yes," Clint said. "No doubt they were killed by the same . . . thing."

"We'd better get goin'," Dakota said. "Now that it's fed, maybe it's headin' for that canyon. Fiddler's there alone."

"Isn't that the way he likes it?" Clint asked.

"It's not the way I like it."

"Maybe there's something in camp we can use."

"I want to get out of here," she said, looking around. "We don't need anythin'."

"All right." He relented. "All right. We should probably bury the . . . the pieces, but we don't have time."

"No, we don't," she said.

They walked back to the horses and mounted up, took one last look at the carnage in the camp, then turned the horses and headed in the direction of the canyon. There was no use following a trail any more.

Fiddler found the entryway to the canyon. He'd missed it last night in the dark. The Wendigo could have gotten by him and into the canyon after its kill. He was going to have to go in and take a look.

On foot.

He tied the packhorse off, left the meager supplies on its back. Then he tied Horse off, but lightly, so if she reared or pulled back she'd be able to get loose.

"The next one could always be the last one, ol' Horse," he said, patting the animal's neck.

He checked his pistol, stuck it back in his belt, then checked the action of his Winchester. Then he touched the leather sack he wore around his neck.

That was where the magic was.

TWENTY-FOUR

"Do you know what a Wendigo does after it's killed or fed?" Clint asked her.

"No," she said. "Fiddler would know."

"There's going to be more hunters traipsing around these woods today," he said. "They might attract it."

"If it went back to that canyon last night, after it killed," she said, "and Fiddler was there . . ."

"We didn't hear any other shots," Clint said. "The Wendigo and Fiddler may have missed each other last night."

"I hope so," she said. "I like that old man. He thinks he can't be killed."

"We can all be killed," Clint said.

"He thinks he has magic that keeps him alive," she said, "magic that kills the Wendigo."

"Well, for his sake," Clint commented, "I hope he's right."

"It may cost me two thousand dollars," she said, "but I hope so, too."

• • •

It was midday by the time Clint and Dakota reached what had obviously been Fiddler's campsite for the night. The fire was cold, but the packhorse and his own horse had been left behind.

"He went into the canyon on foot!" Clint said.

"That crazy old man," Dakota said. "I told you he thinks he can't be killed. He always said the best way to hunt the Wendigo was on foot."

"What, horses and Wendigos don't like each other?" Clint asked. "I thought the Wendigo ate human flesh. Why would they be interested in a horse?"

"I don't know, Clint," she said. "Maybe his mind is actually goin' because of age. Who knows but him?"

"If he went in when he put the fire out, then he's got hours on us," Clint said. "He could be dead already."

"We have to go in," she said. "We have no choice."

"You're the hunter, the sign reader," he said. "You'll be able to tell if it's still in there or not."

"Hopefully," Dakota said.

"What do you mean—hopefully?"

"Remember, Fiddler says the Wendigos are magic," she reminded him. "Maybe they can walk without leaving tracks."

"And maybe they can fly," he said derisively.

"Who knows?"

"I was being sarcastic."

"I know you were," she said, "but . . ."

"Okay," he said, "okay, let's not start thinking these things can fly, all right? Let's at least keep both of our feet on the ground."

"Do you agree we have to go in?"

"Of course," he said. "After all, that's what we're here for. We might as well leave our horses here, too."

They dismounted and tied off their horses. Clint put his hand on the fire, thought he felt some heat still there, so maybe Fiddler didn't have as big a head start as he thought.

On foot they waked to the mouth of the canyon, where Clint waited while Dakota went over the ground. She had to widen her search pattern since the mouth of the canyon was hard and rocky.

"I can see where it came back, probably last night," she said, coming back to him. "And I can see Fiddler's tracks."

"He's an Indian," Clint said. "He leaves tracks?"

"Even he can't step on some brush without flattening it down," she said.

"Okay, so they're both still in there?"

"As far as I can tell, yes."

"Then it's settled," Clint said. "We go in."

"Do we know if this canyon has any other ways in or out?" she asked.

"The sheriff didn't mention it." Clint cursed himself quietly for not having asked.

"We'll just have to hope," she said.

"Yeah," he said. But he didn't know if he was hoping the Wendigo was in there—or not.

Of course, [illegible]

[illegible] as he could.

[illegible]

[illegible]

[illegible]

TWENTY-FIVE

Clint and Dakota entered the mouth of the canyon, which started out wide enough for them to have ridden through side by side, but gradually narrowed. In the end they would not have been able to get their horses through, and would have had to take them back out. It made Clint wonder how a ten-foot Wendigo managed to negotiate the route.

"I can't believe this is the only way in," Dakota said. "There's got to be another, easier way."

"If there is we'll find it," Clint said.

Eventually, the route began to widen again. Clint, looking straight up, realized that at one point it was as if they were in a tunnel. He was not able to see the sky. However, by the time the route widened again the sky was visible.

"At night this whole thing must be like a tunnel," Dakota observed.

Clint just nodded.

Finally, they came out into the interior of the

canyon. It spread out in front of them, causing Clint to say, "This isn't right. Who called this a canyon?"

"What's wrong."

"A canyon," he said, "by definition, is a sort of gorge. It's almost like a scar in the earth—long and deep but not very wide. This is too wide to be called a canyon."

"Well, Fiddler is out there somewhere," Dakota said. "How do we find him?"

"Are we looking for him or the Wendigo?" Clint asked.

"Doesn't make much difference," she said. "Find one and we'll find the other, don't you think?"

Fiddler was surprised at the size of the "canyon" as he entered it earlier that morning. Who had told him it was a canyon? Oh, yes, the sheriff. He doubted the lawman had ever been out here.

As long as a canyon, yes, and as deep, but wider, much wider. More ground to cover than he had originally expected.

The last Wendigo Fiddler had killed had been in Ontario, Canada, near a town called Kenora. It was his fourteenth. This one, when he killed it, would be number fifteen. That one he had found in a cave that eventually became called the Cave of the Wendigo. He looked up at the steep canyons walls and wondered how many caves honeycombed it.

Fiddler was walking the floor of the canyon on foot, tracking as much by instinct and sense of smell as anything else. The canyon floor was hard and rocky, so footprints were at a premium. Here and there a dislodged stone, a trampled bit of growth, but really not much for a conventional tracker to see.

He was not a conventional tracker. Dakota was—and she was also very talented and able to adjust.

Hopefully, she and Clint Adams were not too close on his trail.

"The ground's too hard," Dakota told Clint. "I'm not picking up any definite sign."

"Keep looking," Clint said. "I have faith in you."

Eventually, she began to see what Fiddler had seen and they started to follow.

"Any sign of Fiddler?" Clint asked.

"Not so much as a gob of spit," she said.

"So then we're following the Wendigo."

"For all I know we could be following a bear," she sad. "Not that I think a bear killed those men last night, but we could be following a false trail."

"I'll bet not."

"Why?"

"Have you actually seen any other animals?" Clint asked. "A deer, a jackrabbit? Heard any birds?"

She turned and stared at him.

"No," she said, "now that you mention it. I should've noticed that. They've all cleared out."

"They're afraid," Clint said. "That makes them smart."

"Hey," Dakota said. "I'm afraid. I guess that makes me smart, too."

"Me, too," Clint said. "Good for all of us."

He looked up at the walls.

"I wonder how many caves are around here?"

"Too many to search," she said. "I'll bet they honeycomb the walls on all sides. Let's just hope I'm as good as I think I am and if the Wendigo is in a cave, I can find it."

"I'll bet you are," he said.

She smiled.

"Right now I'd rather be in a hotel room with you."

He laughed.

"That makes two of us."

TWENTY-SIX

The three hunters—Fiddler ahead of Clint and Dakota—spent most of the day wandering the canyon floor, following whatever hint of sign they could find.

"It's getting dark," Dakota said. "Should we turn back?"

"If we do that, we'll have to travel over old ground tomorrow," he said.

"We didn't bring any provisions."

"We can make a fire," Clint said. "I have some beef jerky in my pocket."

She looked around.

"I suppose that'd be the best thing to do."

"What's Fiddler going to do?" Clint asked. "Turn back?"

"Oh, no," she said. "He'll keep goin'. Along with thinkin' he can't die, he also thinks he doesn't have to eat."

"What about drinking?"

"There's plenty of water in here."

They'd passed a couple of water holes over the past few hours.

"All right," Clint said, "let's look for a place to camp. We'll need some wood for a fire."

Ahead of them Fiddler was making camp. The logical thing to do would have been to make a cold camp, but he didn't want to be logical. He wanted to be easy to find. The fire had to be made from brush, and he needed a lot of it to keep it going. He had a canteen over his shoulder, his pistol in his belt, and his rifle between his knees. That was all he needed to wait for the Wendigo.

"It's colder in here than it was outside last night," Dakota complained.

"I noticed that."

Both were wearing jackets, but neither had brought a blanket.

"We'll just have to huddle close together," he said, "for body warmth."

"Just for body warmth?" she asked, moving up close against him.

"Of course." He put his right arm around her, pulled her close. Immediately, he felt her heat. With his left hand he unbuttoned her shirt and slipped his hand inside. He cupped one of her full breasts, felt the heat of her skin and the hardness of her nipple.

"Oh, that helps," he said. "I feel warmer already."

"Not fair," she said. "I'm still cold."

She reached over and undid his trousers, stuck her hand down the front until she could wrap her hand around his hot, thickening penis.

"Ah," she said, "that's better. You know, if we had a blanket we could—"

"Wouldn't that help the Wendigo out?" he asked. "We wouldn't notice it because we were rolling around on a blanket together."

"Oh." She shuddered. "You had to remind me."

They each removed their hands, but remained huddled close.

Fiddler didn't feel the cold.

He did not feel hunger.

And he did not feel fear.

All he felt was anticipation of the kill.

He could smell the Wendigo, and he was sure the Wendigo could smell him and his magic. If that was true, the creature would not come for him tonight. He would have to find it tomorrow.

He drank some water from his canteen, stoppered it, and then folded his arms in front of him, cradling his rifle.

TWENTY-SEVEN

The night went by uneventfully—at least, inside the canyon.

Outside, the area was swarming with hunters eager for the thousand-dollar bounty. Several of them shot each other during the course of the day, giving Sheriff Dekker some disputes to handle. Luckily, no one had been killed . . . yet.

Dekker went to see the mayor the next morning.

"It's gonna get out of hand, Mayor," he said. "They're out there shooting at anythin' that moves."

"What do you want me to do about it?" Payne demanded.

"Take the bounty off," Dekker said. "Give Fiddler, Adams, and the girl a chance to work."

"I can't do that," Payne said. "I have a duty to this town. The more guns that are out there, the more chance there is somebody will get that thing."

"They're gonna kill each other, sooner or later," Dekker said. "How are you gonna explain that?"

"I won't have to," Payne said, "if somebody kills it. That's all people are going to care about."

"This is a mistake, Mayor."

"The only mistake, Dekker, is that you're not out there hunting for it, too."

"I have a duty to this town, too, Mayor," Dekker said. "That means stayin' in town, tryin' to keep people from gettin' killed."

"Then go do your job," the mayor said. "I'm not removing the bounty. In fact, I'm considering raising it."

Dekker opened his mouth to protest, but realized it wouldn't do any good. He turned and stormed out of the mayor's office. When he got to the street, he saw two hunters riding back into town, with a body wrapped in a blanket slung over a third horse. He recognized them as amateur hunters who had come into town yesterday afternoon and gone out just hours later.

"What happened?" he demanded.

"We're not sure," one of then said. "He got killed last night."

"Where?"

"Out there," the other one said.

"I know out there," Dekker said. "Where, exactly."

"We're not sure."

"Take him to the undertaker," Dekker said. "I'll meet you there."

"We need a drink."

"The saloon's not open," Dekker said. "It's too early. The undertaker will have a bottle. Go and stay there until I arrive."

"Sure, Sheriff."

He didn't know if the man had been killed by the

Wendigo or not, but when he saw the unwrapped body he at least wanted to have the town doctor with him for an opinion.

He wondered where Fiddler, Adams, and the girl were, and if they were still alive.

TWENTY-EIGHT

Clint and Dakota each took watch and spent it with the other leaning against them, asleep. It wasn't a good idea, because the person being leaned on ended up with one arm asleep, but they made sure it was not their gun arm.

When they were both awake, they stood and kicked the fire to death.

"What do you think happened last night?" Dakota asked. "Did it go out and kill?"

"Well, it didn't kill us," Clint said. "So unless it killed Fiddler, it must have."

"And it left by going right past us?"

"Around us, more than likely," Clint said, "or out another way. We still don't know if there's just the one way in or out."

"You know," she said, "Fiddler claims he's killed fourteen of these things."

"That's impressive," Clint said, "but I'm sure he'd never claim it was easy."

"He says some myths say the Wendigo, when it turns sideways, is so thin it can't be seen."

"That doesn't make it sound very dangerous."

"Other myths claim they grow as large as fifteen feet."

"Now that sounds dangerous."

They got themselves together and started walking.

Fiddler was not concerned with other ways in or out of the canyon. He knew if the Wendigo wanted to it could scale the walls, or even fly over them. He also knew that the Wendigo would not face him until it wanted to. However, if he could find it when it was at rest, he might be able to force the issue.

Fiddler could feel through his moccasins the ground where the Wendigo had stepped. It was hotter. No other hunters—not even Dakota—could do that. That was why he would find the Wendigo before she did. The only way she could find it first was if she stumbled into it.

It was well into his second day in the canyon when he thought he had at least found where the Wendigo had spent the night. It might not be there now, and it might or might not return, but he had to get a look at it, anyway.

And that meant he had to climb.

"This man was not killed by the same animal that killed the other one," Doctor Milburn said. All the time they'd been in town together the sheriff still only knew the older man as Doc Milburn. He had initials on his shingle—D.E. Milburn—but nobody knew what they meant. "The Lawrence boy was torn apart. This man was simply mauled to death."

"Mauled? By an animal?"

The doctor looked at him.

"Humans don't maul other humans, Sheriff," he said. "Yes, he was killed by an animal. I'd say a big cat of some kind."

"Doc," Dekker said, "we ain't had any indication that there's a big cat in the area."

"Well," Doc said, pointing at the dead man, "you got some now. See those wounds? They're from claws."

"The Wendigo has claws."

Doc held up his hand.

"I don't want to hear anything about a Wendigo. I don't believe in that mumbo-jumbo. When you're around me just keep it to yourself."

"Well, okay," Dekker said, rubbing his jaw, "maybe a big cat would be enough reason for the mayor to remove the bounty—"

"Mayor Payne?" Doc snorted. "That idiot! You tell him there's a cougar loose around here and he'll just put out another bounty. I've already patched up three fool hunters who have been shot by other fool hunters, and this ain't the end of it, believe me."

Doc turned away from the body and looked at Albert, the undertaker.

"Albert, this place is still a pit."

"Yes, Doc."

"I'm warning you," the physician went on. "You don't get it cleaned up I'm going to have you shut down."

"You need me for anything else, Sheriff?" he asked.

"No, Doc, that's it. Thanks."

Doc Milburn left and Albert cackled.

"That old geezer," he said. "He shuts me down and bodies will pile up around here. He ain't gonna shut me down."

Dekker shook his head. One old geezer calling the other one an old geezer.

"Bury him, Albert. Boot hill. No marking."

"Sure thing, Sheriff."

Dekker shook his head and left. If a Wendigo had not killed this man, it was sure a hell of a coincidence that a big cat would come around now.

TWENTY-NINE

One thing Clint noticed was that Dakota had great eyes. Great-looking eyes, sure, but also great eyesight. She spotted sign well before he did, and often had to point it out to him.

This time she didn't spot something on the ground—but something above them.

"There!" she said for a third time, pointing. "Come on, Clint, can't you see? It's Fiddler. He's climbing the rock face."

"That's a long way off, Dakota," he said. "How can you be sure it's Fiddler?"

"Because nobody else would be that darin'," she said, "or stupid. That old man is gonna kill himself."

As they quickened their pace to reach him, Clint said, "He must think there's a cave up there."

"There's caves all over," she said. "He thinks the Wendigo is up there."

"So the Wendigo can also scale a rock wall?" Clint asked. "This thing is getting more and more talented as we go along."

Dakota said something that Clint didn't catch.

"What was that?"

"You probably don't want to hear this," she said, "but Fiddler says they can probably . . . fly."

"Fly," Clint said. "As in . . . like a bird?"

"Yeah."

"How the hell did he ever kill fourteen of them?" Clint wondered aloud.

The wall Fiddler was climbing was steep, without many opportunities for a good handhold and foothold at the same time. He'd had to attach his belt to his rifle and loop it over his neck, and the gun stuck in his belt was getting in the way. It was a dangerous ascent, for more reasons than one. If the Wendigo came for him now, he would be as good as dead. There was no way he could kill it while clinging to the rock wall. Also, there was always the possibility he'd lose his grip and fall. But even then he had confidence that his magic would keep him alive.

And just at that moment a jutting formation he grabbed onto broke away from the wall, crumbling in his hand, and it happened.

He fell.

"Oh, my God!" Dakota said. Clint saw. Fiddler had lost his grip on the wall and was plummeting his arms, windmilling as if he thought he could fly.

"Come on!" she exhorted, and started running.

When they reached the area, she looked around.

"He must've fallen here," she said.

"Are you sure you got the right spot?" Clint asked.

"Yeah," she said, looking up and shading her eyes. "He was climbing the wall here."

"Well, let's look around," Clint said. "He's got to be here someplace."

There were all sorts of rock formations and some brush that could be hiding Fiddler's battered and broken body. They split up to look around. As Clint came around a particularly large rock, he saw Fiddler. The man was standing there, brushing himself off as if he'd just tripped over a rock—but he had fallen almost fifty feet!

"Fiddler?"

The Cree hunter looked up at Clint and smiled.

"Clumsy," he said.

Eric Keller rode into Rosesu that afternoon, straight down Main Street, easy as you please. Dekker was standing outside in front of his office. When he saw Keller, he stepped into the street. Keller reined his horse in. He looked the same, a hard case with a granite jaw and some gray hair that made him look older than forty.

"Whataya want here, Keller?" Dekker asked.

"Why, Sheriff," Keller said. "Come out to greet me all by yourself? Where's your deputy?"

"I ain't had a deputy since you killed the last one," Dekker said. "Four months ago."

"He called me out, Dekker," Keller said. "If you didn't believe that, I'd be behind bars by now."

"But I told you never to come back here."

"I know," Keller said, "and it was my intention to stay away—until I heard about this bounty."

"You don't hunt game, Keller," Dekker said with distaste, "you hunt men."

"I hunt, period," Keller said. "Are you tellin' me I can't go for this bounty?"

"Go ahead," Dekker said. "The forest is swarming with amateurs with guns. I hope one of them takes your head off by accident."

"Nice to see you, too, Troy," Keller said, and rode on.

THIRTY

"Dakota!"

Clint called out and she came running. When she reached him, she gaped at Fiddler, who was still slapping rock dust from his clothing.

"Fiddler!" she exclaimed. "Goddamn it. Fiddler! But . . . but how?"

"I think she means . . . why aren't you dead?"

The old man looked at both of them, then smiled and touched the leather bag around his neck.

"This."

"That's your medicine bag, isn't it?"

"Yes."

"And that saved you?" she asked.

"It slowed my fall."

"So you did fall?" she asked. "We didn't imagine it?"

"Oh, no, I fell," he said. "I landed very hard, too." He stretched, put his hand to his lower back.

"But not hard enough to kill you," Clint said.

Fiddler looked at Clint.

"I was certain Dakota would have told you."

"That you can't die?"

"Oh, I can die," Fiddler said. "Years from now I will die of old age, like most people."

"But . . ."

"But I cannot be killed."

"And that's because of what's in your medicine bag?"

"Yes."

Clint looked at Dakota, who looked up at the face of the wall.

"What were you doin' up there, Fiddler?"

"I believe there is a cave up there," he said, "where the Wendigo rested last night."

"Two hunters were killed last night in their camp," Clint told him. "Torn to pieces."

"Yes," Fiddler said. "I heard the shots . . . and the scream."

"So if the Wendigo made a kill last night, it would rest?" Clint asked.

"It would rest in any case."

Now Clint looked up.

"There's got to be an easier way up there."

"There probably is," Fiddler said, "but it'll be dark soon. We should wait for daylight before we look for it."

"And you should rest," Dakota said.

"Yes," Fiddler said, "you are probably right. We can make camp right here."

"Right below the Wendigo's cave?" Clint asked.

"Why not?" Fiddler asked. "We are looking for it, aren't we?"

"Yes, but—"

"Don't worry," Fiddler said. "The chances are slim that it would come back to the same place."

"Then why did you want to get into it?" Clint asked.

"It is the last place the Wendigo was," Fiddler said. "It would help me to get inside."

"And what if it stays somewhere else tonight?" Clint asked. "Then that would be the last place it stayed. Will you still want to get up there tomorrow morning?"

"Every little bit helps, Mr. Adams," Fiddler said.

"If we're gonna make camp, we better get a fire going," Dakota said.

Fiddler looked around, located his rifle lying on the ground. Then he continued looking.

"What's wrong?"

"My pistol fell from my belt."

"I'll help you find it."

"No," he said, "you help Dakota. I will find it."

"All right," Clint said. "We'll get a fire going. Do you have any food?"

"Some beef jerky."

"I do, too," Clint said. "And water. That'll have to do."

"It will do very well," Fiddler assured him.

"What is it now?" Mayor Payne asked Dekker.

"Keller's in town."

"You told him not to come back."

"Apparently, he didn't listen."

"Why's he here?"

"He says for the bounty."

"He doesn't hunt animals."

"I know."

"Then why do you think he's here?"

"Keller doesn't do anythin' without a reason."

"And what do you think his reason is this time?"

"There's only one reason I can think he would've come back," Dekker said.

"And what's that? Or do I have to guess?"

Dekker looked at Payne and said, "Clint Adams."

THIRTY-ONE

They were all seated around the fire. Clint realized this had to be his and Dakota's last night in the canyon. They couldn't go on without more provisions. He would have thought the same was true of Fiddler, but the old Cree hunter seemed to be doing much better than the two of them, despite his fall.

As they'd collected wood for the fire earlier, Dakota had said, "I don't believe he could've fallen from that height and not gotten killed, or hurt."

"Maybe he landed on some brush," Clint said. "Maybe it broke his fall."

"And maybe he really does have some magic," she said.

Clint didn't have an answer for that.

He and Dakota were chewing beef jerky and taking small sips of water. Fiddler had one swallow of water, and that was it.

"I am used to going without food and water for long periods of time," he told them. "It is what I must do to be able to continue to hunt."

"We'll have to go back in the morning," Clint said.

"I understand."

"We have to find another way into the canyon," he said. "So we can bring horses and provisions."

"You do that, and I will continue to look."

Clint figured Fiddler wanted to get them out of the way—probably to get Dakota out of harm's way.

"Fiddler, wouldn't it be better to look outside the canyon than in?" he asked. "I mean, that's where this thing is doing its killing, right?"

"It would be impossible," Fiddler said, "to kill it while it is killing. I have to find it at rest."

"That would be at night," Clint said. "How are you going to find it at night?"

"Early morning would be good enough," Fiddler said. "At first light is the best time."

"And what if it finds you?" Dakota asked.

"That is just as good."

"Clint, we have to stay," she said.

"I don't know about you, Dakota, but I'm hungry, and I need more than the sips of water we've been taking. We have to go and get supplies, but we can come back."

Dakota turned and looked at Fiddler.

"Come with us, Fiddler," she said. "We'll all come back."

"I will be fine here, child," he told her. "I will be here when you get back."

"Alive?" she asked.

"Very much alive," he promised.

"You'd better be."

• • •

Later, while Dakota slept and Fiddler was supposed to be on watch, Clint came and sat with him at the fire.

"You are not weary?" the Cree asked.

"Weary to my bones, Fiddler," Clint said. "I just wanted to talk to you while Dakota was asleep."

"What about?"

"The Wendigo."

"Why?"

"I like to know about what I'm hunting for," Clint said. "The more I know, the better chance I have."

"That is not the case, here."

"Why not?"

"You have no chance," Fiddler said, "and neither does she."

"Why not?"

"You do not have the magic."

"Your medicine bag?"

Fiddler took the bag into his hand.

"This is my medicine, not my magic," he said. "The magic is here." He touched his chest. "Inside. The medicine bag helps me to focus it. You do not have either."

"And you really do think this is a mythical beast called the Wendigo?"

Fiddler looked at him and shook his head.

"You have even less than no chance if you do not believe," he said.

"Well," Clint said, "I have to admit you have a point there."

"You have seen what it can do?" Fiddler asked.

"Yes," Clint said. "We went to the camp that was attacked last night, found the two men . . . dismembered."

"And still you do not believe?"

"It's . . . hard."

"I will tell you what is even harder."

"What's that?"

"Killin' somethin' you do not believe in."

THIRTY-TWO

In the morning, Clint and Dakota left Fiddler to find another way up the rock wall.

"If I didn't have such an open mind," Clint said to her, as they walked away, "I might think that he was crazy. Just a little."

"A little?"

After they had walked for a while, she turned and looked back, shielding her eyes.

"I'd say he's a lot crazy," she said.

Clint turned and looked.

"Is that—"

"Yup," she said, "he's scalin' the wall . . . again."

In the afternoon, they made their way out of the canyon. It didn't take them as long walking back because they weren't trying to follow a trail. When they came out, the horses were all still standing there.

"We'll have to water them before we ride them too long," Clint said.

"Are we goin' back to town?" she asked.

"No," Clint said. "We have supplies in our saddlebags. Fiddler's got some on his horses. We'll take from him what we can carry, and then start looking for another way into the canyon.

"Do you think there's another way?" she asked.

"We can probably work our way to the top," he said. "You can get in from there."

"But a way to get in with the horses?"

"That's what I'm hoping for."

They raided Fiddler's horses, found that there wasn't much on the packhorse they could use. They did get some beef jerky from his saddlebags, as well as some coffee.

"We should leave some of it here, in case he comes back out this way," Clint said.

"He needs very little," she said.

"Still . . ."

They left some coffee and food in the saddlebags of Horse.

"Too bad we can't water his horses," Clint said.

"We can give them what's in our canteen," she offered. "I can find us more water."

Clint thought it over, then decided to go ahead. Using his hat, they gave water first to Horse and then to the pack animal. That left them with very little at the bottom of one of their canteens.

"We'll have to find water first thing," she said. "The horses need it, and we can fill our canteens."

"Okay," he said as they mounted up. "Lead the way."

That afternoon, Dekker found Keller sitting at a table in the saloon.

"You're not here for the bounty," Dekker said.

"What makes you say that?" Keller asked, looking up at the lawman.

"If you were, you'd be out searching."

"You ain't much of a hunter, are you, Sheriff?"

"Whataya mean?"

"I'm waitin' for the next one or two amateur hunters to be killed," Keller said. "That's where I'll start lookin', at the site of the most recent kill."

"That's cold-blooded."

"That's huntin'. You want a drink?"

"Not with you."

"Suit yourself."

"I'm thinkin' you're here for another reason."

"And what would that be?"

"Reputation."

"Whose?"

"Clint Adams's."

"The Gunsmith? Is he in town?"

"You know he was," Dekker said. "Now he's out there, hunting for the Wendigo."

Keller laughed.

"What's so funny?"

"They got you really believin' there's somethin' out there called a Windy-go?"

"Well, somethin's out there killin' people."

"An animal," Keller said, "pure and simple."

"Not simple," Dekker said. "There's nothin' simple about this."

"So," Keller said, sitting back in his chair, "Clint Adams is in town, huh?"

THIRTY-THREE

Dakota found a water source fairly quickly, a creek that was running clear. The horses drank while Clint filled both canteens and handed one to her.

"I wonder if that old man made it to the top?" she said.

"He wasn't going to the top, just to the cave," Clint reminded her.

"I'm just wonderin' if he fell again," she said. "If he'd even survive another fall."

"Well, apparently he can't be killed, can he?"

She shook her head.

"I guess I never believed it until I saw it with my own eyes."

"But we didn't see it," Clint said. "We didn't see him land, did we?"

"We saw him fall."

"Did we? Was that really him?"

"Who else could it have been?"

"I don't know," Clint said. "I just can't fully accept

that he fell from that wall and didn't suffer even a scratch."

"The medicine bag."

"What about it?"

"Some people say it helps the wearer heal."

"Heal?" Clint asked. "He didn't have time to heal. No, he didn't have a scratch on him."

"Unbelievable, either way," she said.

They placed their canteens on their saddles, led the horses away from the water before they could gorge themselves.

"Where to?" she asked.

"You're asking me?" he said. "I'm not in charge here."

"I don't know what to do, Clint," she said. "I don't want to be in charge anymore."

"Dakota . . . I think maybe we should go back."

"To town?"

He nodded.

"No," she said, shaking her head. "I know I don't want to do that. I want to try to get back to Fiddler."

"Not in charge, huh?" he asked. "You know what you want to do, Dakota. That's being in charge."

"All right," she said. "So we just keep on lookin' for another way in."

"We keep looking."

She stared at him and smiled.

"You knew that, right? That's why you said we should go back. You knew I wouldn't do it."

"I figured."

She shook her head.

"Looks like you already know me better than I

know myself." She sniffed herself then and smiled. "Looks like that bath is finally startin' ta wear off."

Keller thought he could do a double while he was in town. Collect the bounty on whatever this animal was that was terrorizing everyone, and take the name "Keller the Hunter". Soon, he'd be Keller, the man who killed the Gunsmith.

He'd had no idea when he rode into town that Clint Adams was anywhere in the area. He was going to have to thank the sheriff for the information. Maybe buy him a drink. Yeah, that was it, he'd buy the lawman a drink.

"Hey," somebody shouted into the saloon, "they just brought in another body!"

Keller smiled. Time to go to work.

Sheriff Dekker stepped out into the street to meet the man who was leading a second horse with a body slung over it.

"What happened?"

The man just stared at him, glassy-eyed.

"What's goin' on?" Keller asked.

"Make yerself useful, Keller," Dekker said, moving to the second horse. "Drag that poor bastard off his horse and get him over to Doc's."

"Sure, Sheriff," Keller said. "Always glad to help."

As a crowd gathered, Dekker untied the ropes holding the body on the second horse, then pulled back the blanket it was wrapped in. He exposed the face, which had been torn open by claws.

"Win-dee-go," somebody whispered.

"Looks more like the work of a cougar," Dekker said, covering the face. He turned, picked somebody out. "Dusty, take this fella over to the undertaker's place."

"Sure, Sheriff."

Dekker turned, saw Keller leading the other man away on foot, toward Doc's. Keller was also talking to the man, probably getting whatever information he could. That was fine with Dekker. If Keller killed or got killed, both would work for him.

THIRTY-FOUR

Clint and Dakota found another camp that had been hit. There was blood everywhere, but no bodies. Dakota walked around, studying the ground, and decided she knew what had happened.

"The camp got hit and somebody survived, took the other body or bodies away on another horse. One other body, I think. Looks like two horses."

"This thing is hitting once a night now." Clint noted. "We're getting up in the double figures for dead bodies."

"It's got to be stopped," she said. "We've got to get back to Fiddler, Clint."

"Let's keep riding," Clint said. "If there's another way into that canyon . . ."

"And if there's not?" she asked.

"Then we just have to hope that Fiddler is the one who comes out of there alive."

"Hope?" she asked. "Or pray?"

"Let's do both . . ."

• • •

Keller came out of the doctor's office, saw Dekker waiting for him.

"You goin' out?" Dekker asked.

"Yep, right now."

"I'm comin' with you."

"Why?"

"Because I've been sittin' around here long enough," Dekker said. "I may not be able to kill some magical beast, but maybe I can get the cougar that killed this man and the one yesterday."

"Suit yourself," Keller said. "I'm goin' to saddle my horse right now."

"I'll get some supplies," Dekker said, "and meet you at the livery."

Dekker came out of the general store with a sack of supplies, ran right into Mayor Payne.

"What's going on?" the mayor asked. "I heard there was another body brought in."

"You heard right."

"This town's going crazy, Dekker," Payne said. "People running around and into each other like chickens with their heads cut off." He noticed the sack. "Where are you off to?"

"I'm gonna do my job," Dekker said. "Keller's goin' after that thing and I'm goin' with him."

"You and Keller? Is that wise?"

"I got to do somethin'."

"Yes, but Keller . . . would you even be going with him if he wasn't—"

"Don't say it, Mayor," Dekker said, cutting the man off. "Just don't say it."

"What do we do for law while you're gone?" Payne asked.

"Appoint a deputy," Dekker said. "Or better yet, strap on a gun and pin a badge on yourself."

"Who," Payne asked, "would you advise I appoint as a deputy in your absence?"

Dekker met Keller in front of the livery.

"Feller in there told me this was your horse, so I saddled it," Keller said.

"Thanks."

Dekker tied the sack to his saddle horn, slid his rifle into the scabbard, and mounted up.

"What's in the sack?"

"Just some jerky and coffee," Dekker said. "And some extra shells."

"Everythin' we need," Keller said, swinging into his saddle.

"Keller, this don't mean that anythin's changed between us," Dekker said.

"I know it."

"Okay, just wanted to make sure."

"Just don't get in my way if we find Clint Adams first," Keller advised.

"Hey," Dekker said, "if you want to get killed, don't let me stop you."

"You think he's that good?"

"He's got the rep."

"I got a rep."

"Not like his."

"How old is he now, anyway?"

Dekker gigged his horse forward and said, "Old enough, I guess."

THIRTY-FIVE

"Look," Clint said.

Dakota stared ahead, where Clint was pointing.

"A cliff?" she asked.

"Maybe . . ."

They rode up to it, dismounted, and walked to the edge. They found themselves looking down into the canyon.

"Long way down," he said.

They could see how far the canyon spread in either direction.

"It's more of a valley than a canyon," Clint said, looking down at it from above.

"I can't see Fiddler," she said.

"Come on," he said. "If we ride along this ridge, maybe we can find a way down."

"How would we find him down there?" she asked. "How would we find our way back to that cave, where we left him?"

"I don't know," Clint said. "But before we can worry about that, we've got to find a way down."

"All right," she said, remounting, "let's go."

They'd only ridden a short way when Dakota said, "Wait."

"What is it?"

She dismounted. Went down to one knee and studied the ground.

"Tracks?" he asked.

She looked back at him over her shoulder.

"We've got a big cat in the area," she said.

"Great," he said, "that's all we need."

She mounted up and looked at him.

"At least we know a cat can be killed by a bullet."

"Yeah," he said, "unless it's a magic cat."

"Don't even think that," she said.

"Okay," Dekker said, "you're the big tracker. Go ahead and track."

Keller dismounted, walked the ground ahead of him for a few seconds, then turned to look up at Dekker.

"What do you want me to track?"

"Whataya mean?"

"I've got tracks from horses," Keller said.

"Forget that. They could've been made by anybody."

"I've got sign that something very big passed by here."

"How big?"

"Real big," Keller said. "Bigger than a grizzly."

"And what else?"

"Paw prints," Keller said.

"Cougar?"

"Looks like it."

"Damn it," Dekker said. "Cougars don't usually attack humans, do they?"

"Not normally," Keller said. "They're hunt-and-prey specialists. They'll stalk somethin' for a long time before they finally attack it, and then usually only for food."

"Then why's this one attacking men?"

"I don't know," Keller said, "but I'll tell you something else. They're very territorial. They won't even compete with a wolf for hunting ground. They'd rather look somewhere else. You've got somethin' else at work here, somethin' big. I don't know why a big cat would choose to hunt here, especially now."

"What would be your guess?"

Keller stared up at Dekker and said, "This ain't no normal cat."

"What now?" Clint asked.

"The cat," she said.

"What about it?"

She turned in her saddle and looked at him.

"I think it knows the way in and out of the canyon."

"Valley," Clint said.

"What?"

"It's a valley," Clint said. "The Valley of the Wendigo."

"Well," Dakota said, "whatever ya wanna call it, the cat knows the way."

"Unusual," Clint said, "for a cat to share its hunting ground like this."

"This whole situation is unusual," Dakota pointed out.

"More for me than for you," Clint said. "At least you've dealt with Fiddler before. I haven't dealt with anything like this before."

"You'd better hope you don't have to do it again, Clint," she told him.

"I will," Clint said, "if we come out of this alive."

THIRTY-SIX

Fiddler could smell the cat.

He had stayed in the Wendigo cave as long as he could, but after a while there was nothing left there for him. No hint of the Wendigo anymore. Time to go and look elsewhere.

Back on the valley floor he saw the sign of the cat. Like the others before him—Keller and Dekker, Clint and Dakota—he knew that this was no ordinary cat.

The cougar was also a ghost walker. It taught spiritual leadership. Was the cat here, he wondered, to help him kill the Wendigo?

Or for reasons of its own?

"Well, I'll be."

Dakota turned to look at Clint, then pointed with a big smile on her face.

"I told you," she said. "Follow the trail of the cat and he'd lead us to the valley."

They both looked down at the path. It wound along

the steep wall, and if they and their horses could walk it, they'd go all the way down to the valley floor.

"We don't know how much it thins out," Clint said. "We bring our horses, we're taking a chance of getting stuck."

"And if we leave them, we have the same problem as before. I say we take the chance."

"Okay," Clint said. "We'll ride them as far as we can, walk them when we have to."

"We should have brought Fiddler his horse," she said.

"No," Clint said. "If Fiddler goes back out the way he came in, he'll want to find his horse there."

"You're probably right."

Clint looked down.

"I'll go first," he said. "Eclipse is bigger than your horse. If he can make it, then so will you."

"Mine's pretty sure-footed."

"Good," Clint said, "then we shouldn't have any trouble at all, should we?"

Keller stopped.

"What is it?" Dekker asked.

"Let's follow the cat," Keller said.

"Why?"

"Because we know it's real."

Dekker looked around. He was surprised that he hadn't heard any shots since they left town. It looked like the Wendigo and the cat had convinced all the amateurs to stay away.

"Fiddler is still out there," he said. "Adams and the girl, too. They're lookin' for that goddamned Wendigo."

"Okay," Keller said. "We let them have it, and we take the cat. Or maybe . . ."

"Maybe what?"

"Maybe the cat will lead us to the Win-dee-go."

Clint told himself not to look down, but he did. Every time Eclipse's hoof knocked a rock or a stone over the edge, he looked down and watched it fall.

He could hear Dakota breathing hard behind him. Ever since he'd seen her look up the rock face where Fiddler had fallen, he had the feeling she was afraid of heights. Her heavy breathing was convincing him he was right.

"You okay back there?" he asked.

"I'm fine," she said tightly.

At one point the ledge grew smaller and they decided to dismount and walk the horses.

"Just don't look down."

"Like you?"

"Yeah," he said. "Like me."

Fiddler heard something from above, stopped, and looked up. Could have been the Wendigo, or the cat, but instead he saw two people on horseback, negotiating a thin path down. He shook his head in admiration. They had found themselves another way into the valley.

THIRTY-SEVEN

Clint and Dakota had to walk the horses the rest of the way down. When they got there, they found themselves looking at Fiddler, who did not look any the worse for wear. He was seated on a rock, staring at them.

"What took you so long?" the old Cree asked.

Dakota gaped at him, speechless.

"How did you know where we'd be?" Clint asked.

"I didn't," Fiddler said. "You've been dropping rocks on my head for the past half hour."

"This isn't possible," Dakota said.

"Everything is possible, my child."

"Old man, you're gonna tell me that some . . . magic has brought us together at the same place and time?"

"I am not tellin' you anythin'," Fiddler said. "But look." He stood on his feet and spread his arms out. "Here we are. Did you bring some water?"

Clint handed him a canteen.

"Thank you."

Clint dug out a piece of beef jerky and also handed that to the old hunter. Fiddler nodded his thanks, accepted the dried meet in exchange for the canteen.

"Did you get to that cave?" Clint asked.

"Yes, I did," Fiddler said. "The Wendigo had left nothin' behind for me."

"Well, we have another problem."

"The ghost cat."

"Is that what it is?" Clint asked. "Well, why not another mythical creature?"

"This is good," Fiddler said.

"What's good about it?" Dakota asked.

"I will continue to hunt the Wendigo," Fiddler said, "and you can hunt the cat."

"I don't like that," Dakota said. "It still leaves you alone with the Wendigo."

"That is how it must be for me to kill it," Fiddler said. He looked at Clint. "You understand, don't you?"

"I don't understand any of this," Clint said, "but I'm willing to go along with you, Fiddler."

"Clint!"

He turned to face her.

"Sorry, but I'm convinced he knows what he's doing."

"I believe the Wendigo and the cat are both in this valley," Fiddler said, apparently having also decided that it was not a canyon, as they had been told.

"What would happen if they met up with each other?" Clint asked.

"I do not know," Fiddler said. "It would depend on the magic each possesses—"

"What would happen if the Wendigo met up with a normal mountain lion?" Clint asked. "No magic."

"The Wendigo would tear it to shreds," Fiddler said. "But we already know this is not a normal cat. If it were, it would not step one paw into this valley."

"There's got to be something we can do to find these things," Clint said. "Or to make them find us."

"That is true," Fiddler said. "If the Wendigo has been active every night, I have a feeling the amateur hunters will be staying away now."

"Meaning?"

"Meaning it will either have to go to town for its prey," Fiddler said, "or come after us."

"Will it come after you?" Dakota asked. "I mean, wouldn't your magic keep it away?"

Fiddler shook his head.

"If the Wendigo wants me, it will come," he said. "It respects only its own magic."

"Then maybe that's what we should do," Clint said. "Wait for one or both of them to come for us."

"How do we attract them?" Dakota asked.

"How did anyone attract them?" Clint asked. "By making camp, lighting a fire . . . and waiting."

He looked at Fiddler.

"That could work."

"We can try it tonight," Clint said. "The next few nights. We have enough water and beef jerky—"

"I eat and drink very little," Fiddler told him.

"Where should we camp?" Dakota asked.

"I know of a place," Fiddler said. "Come with me. You both need rest."

THIRTY-EIGHT

They camped, built a fire. Clint had some beans and a pan in his saddlebags, so they had beans, jerky, and coffee.

"If the fire don't attract them," Dakota said, "the smell will."

"The cat, maybe," Clint said.

"It will attract the Wendigo," Fiddler said. "When it comes, you must both stay back, understand? The battle will rage between the creature and me."

"And the cat?"

"It's open season on the cat," Fiddler said. "You can take your best shot."

"And if our best shot ain't good enough?" Dakota asked. "If the damned thing is magic?"

"Then I will kill it."

"Sounds to me like you could end up doing all the work, Fiddler," Clint said.

"I am used to doin' all the work, my friend."

Keller and Dekker found Fiddler's horses at the entrance to the canyon. The cat's trail led right inside.

"Ever been in there?" Keller asked.

"No."

"That where you think this Win-dee-go is?"

"That's where they say it goes after it's killed."

"These are Fiddler's animals?"

"Yep."

"Then he's in there."

"Probably."

"And who else?"

"Clint Adams and a girl called Dakota."

"I know Dakota," Keller said. "I've met her. And I know of Fiddler."

"And of the Gunsmith."

"Oh, yeah," Keller said. "I know him." He looked up. "Gettin' dark. Why don't we camp here and go in in the mornin'?"

"The Wendigo kills at night."

"Then maybe we'll catch it goin' in or comin' out."

"Sounds like as good a plan as any," Dekker said.

The dismounted, unsaddled their horses, and made a fire. Over coffee and beans Keller asked, "I wonder why Fiddler went in on foot."

"Maybe the way gets too narrow for the horses," Dekker said.

"That'd be crap," Keller said. "Any other way in?"

"I know of one," Dekker said.

"And you've never used it?"

"No."

"Where is it?"

"Not far," Dekker said. "It's a tunnel."

"Too narrow for the horses?"

"I've heard not."

"So you know men who have been in there?"

"Yes."

"How many?"

"One," Dekker said.

"One?"

"That's all that's ever been in and come out again," Dekker told him.

"And who was that?"

"Doesn't matter," Dekker said. "He's dead now."

Keller stared across the fire at Dekker.

"Tell me somethin,' Dekker."

"What?"

"What are you afraid of? I know you ain't afraid of me. You ain't afraid of some mountain lion."

"No."

"You afraid of the Win-dee-go?"

"I'm not a fool," Dekker said. "Of course I'm afraid."

"But it's just a story," Keller said. "Whatever is killin' around here, there's no magic attached to it. You'll see. All it will take is a bullet."

"I hope you're right."

"A bullet for the cat," Keller said, "a bullet for the Win-dee-go, and a bullet for the Gunsmith."

"The Gunsmith," Dekker said. "Now there's somebody I'd be afraid of if I were you."

"There's a difference between fear and caution, Dekker," Keller said. "I'll be cautious about all three, but I'm not afraid of any of them."

"Makes you a better man than me, I guess."

Dekker picked up the coffeepot. Keller held out his cup and Dekker filled it, then his own.

"No," Keller said, regarding the man over his cup, "not a better man, Dekker, just . . . different."

THIRTY-NINE

The valley was pitch-black all around them. The fire was small, so the circle of light from the flame was small as well.

"If it comes," Dakota said, "it'll come out of the dark fast."

"That's the story that's being told," Clint said. "It comes fast and before you know it you're ripped to shreds, like the Lawrence boy."

"None of them were ready," Fiddler said. "We are ready. I am ready."

Suddenly, they heard a sound from the darkness—a cry. And then again.

"That's the cat," Dakota said.

Clint nodded. He knew the sound made by a hungry cat.

"He won't come near the fire," he said.

"It shouldn't come near the fire," Dakota said.

"That is right," Fiddler said, "but then it should also not even be in this valley."

The cat cried out again.

Closer.

Clint stood up.

"It's circling us," Dakota told him. "Checkin' us out."

"That is the difference between the cat and the Wendigo," Fiddler said. "The cat will not come into camp."

"Well," Clint said, "maybe one of us should go out and get it."

Dakota stood up.

"I'll go," she said. "This is what I do."

"No, I'll go," Clint said.

Fiddler stood up, put his hand on Clint's arm.

"Let her go."

Dakota picked up her rifle, smiled at both men, and then melted into the darkness.

"Now," Fiddler said, taking his hand off Clint's arm, "now you go."

Clint nodded, picked up his rifle, and went after Dakota.

Alone by the fire Fiddler kicked dirt on it, extinguishing it. It became completely dark on the floor of the valley. There was only a sliver of moon, but soon his eyes—along with Clint's and Dakota's—would be used to the darkness.

Fiddler hunkered down to wait.

Clint could hear the cat prowling around and growling at the same time. He couldn't hear Dakota, though. She was that good. He was aware that Fiddler had put out the fire. The Cree hunter was now waiting in the dark for the Wendigo.

They were all in the dark.

Dakota could hear the cat ahead of her, and someone behind her—probably Clint. Hopefully, not the Wendigo.

She watched for the cat's eyes. They would pick up the light from even the sliver of a moon that was above them, and then she'd have it.

She was crouched, rifle gripped tightly in her hands. Once upon a time she used to grip her weapon loosely as a way to force herself to relax, but years ago her prey—a wolf—had hit her from behind, and her rifle had gone flying from her hands. She'd had to kill it with a knife, not without paying the price. Since then she made sure she gripped her weapon tightly.

It was about as dark as Clint had ever experienced. Some clouds had moved and blocked the slice of moon in the sky, and now there was no light at all. Clint knew the cat's eyes could be seen in the dark, so he was on the lookout for them. He'd fire as soon as he saw those eyes. There was no danger that he'd be shooting at Dakota or Fiddler by mistake.

He couldn't hear the cat anymore, but suddenly he heard a sound behind him, from the direction of the camp.

It chilled his blood because he had never heard a sound like that before—from man nor beast.

The sound of a Wendigo.

• • •

Fiddler heard it, but even before that he smelled the foul stench of it.

He turned, took his medicine bag in his left hand, and waited.

Clint wasn't sure what to do. Go forward to help Dakota with the cat? Or back to help Fiddler with the Wendigo? The old Cree had been saying right from the beginning, he had to be alone to kill it. And hadn't Clint just finished telling Dakota he thought the old man knew what he was doing?

Clint moved forward.

FORTY

Thank God cats had claws, Dakota thought.

Off to her left she heard them, *tap-tap-tapping* on whatever stone the cat was walking on. Then they were gone . . . and there again.

And she thought she could hear the big cat breathing. Her sen`ses were that attuned when she was hunting.

Come on, she thought, *come on* . . . her eyes were completely attuned to the darkness now. She thought she could see something moving just ahead of her. And then there they were, the eyes, glowing in the dark, coming toward her . . .

She raised the rifle and fired.

Clint was almost behind Dakota when she fired her rifle. The muzzle flash lit up the night and he could see the cat in flight, leaping at her. Even as her bullet struck the cat, it kept coming. Clint raised his rifle and fired, catching the cat in midair. It continued its forward motion and crashed into Dakota, taking her down. Clint dropped his rifle, drew his gun, and fired, again and again, lighting up the scene sò that he could see where to put each shot. The cat never made a sound, not even with the impact of each shot striking it.

Dakota scrambled out from beneath the cat just as Clint fished a match out of his pocket and struck it. From the light cast by the tiny flame, they could see the cat lying on its side, its breathing labored.

"Jesus," she said. "We hit it—what—five or six times and it's still breathing."

Clint walked to it and delivered one final shot to the head.

"Not anymore," he said.

They heard a blood-curdling scream from behind them. As they turned, Clint scooped up his rifle and they ran for the camp.

The Wendigo came into camp, straight at Fiddler, yellow eyes glazing. Its long teeth were dripping saliva as it screamed, but the Cree hunter stood his ground. When the creature was close enough for him to feel its hot, fetid breath on him, for him to smell its death stench body odor, he knew he had it.

When Clint and Dakota reached the dark camp, they stopped to listen.

Nothing.

"I'm going to relight the fire," Clint said.

"Why did he put it out?" Dakota complained.

Clint used a couple of matches to get the fire going again, and as the circle of light spread out, he expected to see disembodied limbs and a lot of blood. Instead, they saw nothing.

Dakota walked around, looking at the ground.

"There's not even a sign of a struggle here, Clint," she said, turning around and around. "Look at it."

"I'm looking."

"We heard the scream," Dakota said. "It was the Wendigo. It wasn't a human scream."

He said nothing.

"Besides, Fiddler would never scream."

"You've told me that before."

"I stand by it," she said. "The Wendigo screamed . . . but where is it? And where's Fiddler? Look, no rifle, no gun, no knife. It's as if he just disappeared."

Clint was looking around, saw everything for himself that Dakota was talking about.

"We killed the cat," she said. "Did he kill the Wendigo? Or did it kill him and drag him off?"

"No drag marks."

"Then it carried him off."

"There's no blood."

"Then it took him alive."

"You know him," Clint said. "Would he let the Wendigo take him alive?"

"No."

She looked around, then spread her arms and dropped them to her sides uselessly.

"What do we do now?" she asked.

He took his gun out of his holster and said, "Reload."

[illegible]

FORTY-ONE

At first light they searched the area again. Still no sign of a struggle or of blood. Fiddler had disappeared.

"Did he walk off?" Dakota asked. She looked tired, having not slept a wink all night, waiting for the Wendigo to swoop in on them. "Would he do that?"

"It was his idea to douse the fire," Clint pointed out. "Maybe that was so he could sneak off."

"No," Dakota finally decided, "he wouldn't. And remember that . . . shriek? That was the Wendigo."

"I'm going to check on that cat."

Clint walked to where they'd left the body of the cat. There was some blood, but the cat was gone. He returned to camp and told Dakota.

"You shot it in the head," she said. "I saw you."

"I know."

"What do we do now?"

"I'll tell you what I want to do," Clint said.

"What's that?"

"I want to get out of this valley."

She looked around helplessly, then said, "Yeah, okay, let's get out of here."

They were riding back to where they had met up with Fiddler so they could take the same path back up and out of the valley when they spotted two riders coming toward them.

"Who the hell—" Dakota said.

Clint saw the sunlight reflect off a badge on a man's shirt.

"That's the sheriff."

"Who's that with him?"

"We'll find out."

As the riders approached, Clint and Dakota reined in. Sheriff Dekker waved to them.

"Glad to see the two of you alive," he said. "Where's Fiddler?"

"Gone," Clint said.

"Gone . . . where?"

"We don't know," Dakota said. "Last night Clint and I got the cat. Fiddler was in camp, and then he wasn't. And we heard the . . . the shriek of the Wendigo."

"Shriek?" the other man asked.

"This is Keller," Dekker said, with no further explanation.

"The Wendigo," Dakota said. "It had to be."

"So Fiddler's gone and so is the Wendigo?" Dekker asked.

"And the cat?" Keller asked.

"Yes," Clint said.

"Where are you goin' now?" Dekker asked.

"We want to get out of this valley," Dakota said. "It's not . . . right in here."

"We used a path from the top to get in," Clint said. "The way Fiddler came in was too narrow for the—say, how did you get in with your horses?"

"We used another way," Dekker said. "Far end of the valley."

"Valley," Clint said, "not a canyon."

"Can you lead us out?" Dakota asked.

"Sure thing."

"Then do it," she said. "The sooner we get out of this place the better."

"Wait," Keller said. "Is the Wendigo thing dead?"

"We don't know," Clint said, "but you can wait around to find out if you want." He turned and looked at Dekker. "Why didn't you tell me there was another way in?"

"You never asked," Dekker said.

Dekker showed them the way out, and then they headed for town. Keller rode up ahead with Dakota while Dekker lay back with Clint.

"I want to warn you about Keller," Dekker said.

"I've heard of him," Clint said.

"He's looking to pad his rep at your expense," Dekker said. "First he wanted the bounty, and then you. Now that the bounty might be done . . ."

"I get it," Clint said. "What's your connection with him?"

"I ran him out of town a few weeks ago."

"Why?"

"He killed my deputy."

"And you didn't lock him up?"

"It was a fair fight," Dekker said. "That was a case of my fool deputy lookin' to make a name for hisself, so he took off his badge and called Keller out. Keller killed him slicker'n snot."

"He's good, huh?"

"He's good."

"I guess he doesn't have much respect for the law if he came back after you kicked him out."

"Not the law," Dekker said, "just me. He never did respect me, not even when we was kids."

"Kids?"

Dekker nodded.

"Yeah, Keller's my older brother."

FORTY-TWO

When they got back to town, they all rode to the livery to unsaddle their horses and leave them in the care of the liveryman. Clint kept a wary eye on Keller, who didn't seem to be paying any attention to him. He was too busy talking to Dakota.

"Do they know each other?" Clint asked Dekker.

"Yeah," Dekker said, "they know each other. Don't worry, Dakota's too smart to have anything to do with Keller."

Keller left the stable first. By the time Clint, Dekker, and Dakota got outside, he was gone.

"Be on the lookout for him," Dakota warned Clint.

"The sheriff already told me," Clint said. "Thanks."

As they walked back to town together, Dekker asked Clint to come to his office to talk about what had happened.

"I'm gonna have to make a report to the mayor and the town council."

"I'm gonna get a drink," Dakota said. "I'll see you in the saloon."

Clint agreed, and followed Dekker back to his office.

Dakota walked over to the Border Saloon, still going over in her mind the events of the night before. She hated the thought that Fiddler might have been carried off and then killed. And if that was the case, then the Wendigo was still alive and kicking, and would strike again when it got dark.

If it didn't, would that mean Fiddler had killed it? Or would it stop killing on its own?

Dakota had a definite need for some whiskey. But as she entered the saloon, the shock of what she saw stopped her dead in her tracks.

"I put a bullet in the cat's head," Clint was finishing his story. "But in the morning, it was gone."

"Could the carcass have been carried off by another predator?" Dekker asked.

"What other predator carries off a cougar?"

"Coyote? Wolf?"

"Any sign of those around here since the Wendigo?"

"None," Dekker agreed. "So maybe the Wendigo took it."

"After it took Fiddler?"

"I don't know," Dekker said helplessly. "What am I supposed to tell the mayor?"

"Tell him to pick up a damned gun and go hunting," Clint said.

Dekker was about to answer when the door to the office slammed open and Dakota appeared out of breath.

"Ya gotta come . . ." she said.

"What's wrong—" Clint started, but she wouldn't let him ask any questions.

"Ya gotta come," she said again.

Clint exchanged a look with Dekker, who got up from his desk.

"If we gotta come, we gotta come," he said to Clint. "Lead the way, gal."

She was out the door and they had to rush to follow . . .

Dakota led them to the saloon, then stood outside and said, "Have a look."

"What's gotten into you?" Clint asked.

"Just go in and take a look and you'll see."

Clint shrugged. He and Dekker went through the batwing doors into the saloon.

"What the hell—" Dekker said.

"I'll be damned," Clint said.

Sitting at a table alone, except for a half-finished bottle of whiskey, was Jack Fiddler, looking none the worse for wear.

Dakota came in behind them.

"He always gets drunk after a successful hunt," she said.

"Successful, huh?" Clint asked.

"Then the Wendigo is dead?" Dekker asked.

"Ask him," Dakota said, "when he sobers up."

FORTY-THREE

Clint woke the next morning with Dakota—freshly bathed the night before—smelling sweet in the bed next to him, despite the fact that they had worked up a sweat during the night.

The first time he entered her last night, it was as if they were both reveling in the fact that they were alive. He fucked her hard, slamming the bed against the wall again and again while she grunted and moaned beneath him, calling his name, imploring him on and on, harder and harder . . .

. . . later, when they woke, Clint straddled her from behind, kissed her butt cheeks and thighs until she woke up, then turned her over and buried his face in her fragrant bush. He licked her until the bed was wet with her juices, then straddled her and took her again, but slower this time—long, slow strokes that made her grunt in a different way each time he went in to the hilt. He kissed her, kissed her lips and breasts and nipples until she bit her lips to keep from crying out, and then he exploded into her . . .

. . . and later still when he woke he was already erect and in her mouth, and she sucked him like he was sugar-coated until he could hold back no longer and she laughed afterward as she licked her lips and smiled . . .

. . . and then they slept.

The next morning—sober as a judge after a good night's sleep—Jack Fiddler claimed that he killed the Wendigo that night in the valley, and then left.

"I had no reason to stay after the job was done," he reasoned.

"Letting us know you weren't dead," Clint said, "how was that for a reason?"

"You had your own problems with the cat," Fiddler said. "You did kill the cat, didn't you?"

"I think so."

"You think?"

Clint explained what had happened.

"The ghost spirit left the cat and took the body with it," Fiddler said. "You killed it, Clint."

Clint felt oddly relieved to have his kill verified by the master hunter himself.

Most of the day was spent prying the bounty out of the mayor's hands.

"I have no proof," he complained. "No body."

"It was a Wendigo," Fiddler said, when the word was passed to him by the sheriff.

The mayor still complained he could not pay a bounty without proof.

"Okay," Dekker offered, "how about tonight? If we go tonight without a kill, will that prove it?"

"No," the mayor said, "one night won't prove it."

Dekker went back to Fiddler.

"I will not stay more than one night," the Cree said. "If I do not have my money tomorrow, I will bring the Wendigo back."

"You'll what?" Dekker asked.

"I will bring the Wendigo back to life and set it loose again," Fiddler said.

"I'll tell that to the mayor," Dekker said, "and see if it works."

Later, in the saloon, Dekker told Clint and Dakota, "Fiddler's gone."

The three of them were standing at the bar with mugs of beer in their hands.

"I know," she said, "he said good-bye."

"How did you get the mayor to pay him?" Clint asked.

"I didn't," Dekker said. "Fiddler did."

"How?"

"He threatened to bring that thing back to life and set it loose on the town again."

"And that scared the mayor?" Clint asked.

"Let's say it convinced him."

"Could he do that?" Clint asked, looking at Dakota. "Could he bring it back to life?"

"You're askin' me that like you actually believe it was alive in the first place," she said, looking amused.

"Well . . . something was alive in that valley," Clint said, "and it looks like Fiddler got rid of it."

"Well," she said, "I wouldn't put it past that old man, would you?"

"Not me," Clint said. "I wouldn't put anything past him."

He looked at the sheriff.

"Me, neither," the lawman said. "I'm just glad it's all over."

"Almost over," Clint said, nodding his head toward the door.

Dekker and Dakota looked in that direction and saw that Keller had entered the saloon.

"Goddamn it," Dekker said.

Keller approached them and Dekker made his feelings known even louder.

"Goddamn it, Keller!"

"This ain't got nothin' to do with you, Dekker."

"The hell it ain't."

"Hey, if you two are brothers," Clint asked, "why do you have different last names?"

"I changed mine," Dekker said. "I took my maw's last name after Keller, here, killed his first man."

"That was a long time ago," Keller said. "We wuz kids."

"The man you killed was no kid," Dekker said. "As I recall he was a family man."

"He pushed me into a fight," Keller said. "He got what he deserved."

"So now you want to push me into a fight?" Clint asked.

"That's what we do, you and me," Keller said to Clint.

"You and me?" Clint asked. "How old are you, Keller?"

"Thirty-five."

"You aren't in the same class as me, boy," Clint said. "I know your reputation. It's been built on killing farmhands, and store clerks, and foolish young deputies."

Keller's face turned red.

"You think so?"

"I know so," Clint said, "so go away and let me finish my beer with my friends."

Clint turned his back on Keller, a move that made both Dekker and Dakota cringe.

Keller glared at Clint's back for a few moments, then his shoulders and back settled down and he asked, "You mind if I have a beer with ya?"

"That's up to your brother," Clint said.

"One beer," Keller said, "and then you and me is goin' out onto the street. I'll show you a reputation built on farmers."

Clint turned again and looked at the man.

"Okay, I'll tell you what. I'm going to buy you a beer."

Clint signaled to the bartender to bring him two fresh beers.

"You stand at that end of the bar," Clint said, "I'll stand at this end."

Dekker grabbed Dakota's arm and pulled her away so that no one was standing between Keller and Clint.

"What's he doin'?" she asked.

"One beer is Clint, the other one is Keller," Dekker explained. "I seen this once before."

"You make the first move," Clint said. "Let's see who can shoot the other beer first."

"This is stupid."

"You shatter my beer before I shatter yours," Clint said, "and I'll step out into the street with you."

"And if you shatter mine?"

"Then you're dead," Clint said, "so to speak."

Keller looked around the room, saw that everyone was watching him expectantly.

"Okay?" Clint asked.

"Okay."

Clint pushed one beer down the bar to Keller, who caught it with his left hand.

"When you're ready," Clint said.

Keller dropped his left hand from the body, dangled his right near his gun. When he went for his weapon, the beer mug next to him suddenly shattered, dousing him with beer. He stared at Clint Adams, whose gun was already back in his holster. Keller had never even cleared leather.

Dekker and Dakota rejoined Clint at the bar, and Dekker said, "Bartender, give my brother a fresh beer. I think he needs it."

Watch for

FIVE POINTS

318th novel in the exciting GUNSMITH series
from Jove

Coming in June!

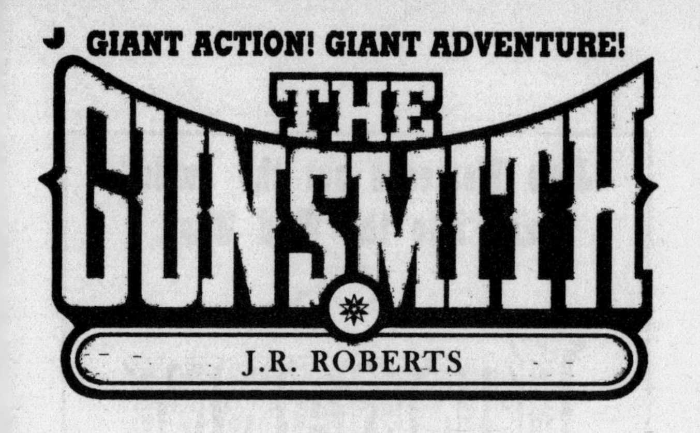
GIANT ACTION! GIANT ADVENTURE!
THE
GUNSMITH
J.R. ROBERTS

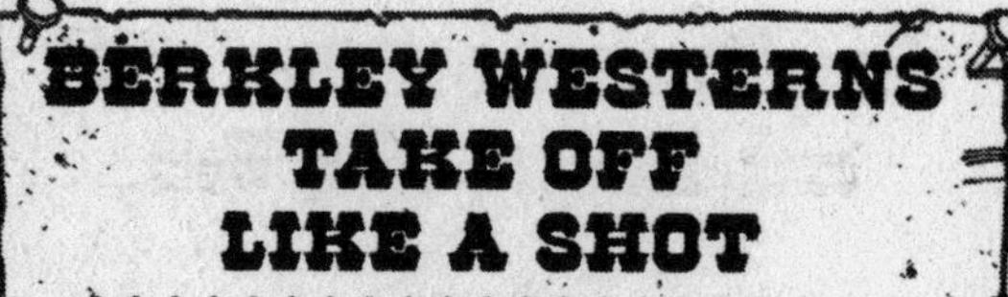

LYLE BRANDT

PETER BRANDVOLD

JACK BALLAS

J. LEE BUTTS

JORY SHERMAN

ED GORMAN

MIKE JAMESON